D1333328

30130501336639

MISTY AND THE
SINGLE DAD

MISTY AND THE SINGLE DAD

BY

MARION LENNOX

MILLS
BOON®

First published in Great Britain 2011
by Mills & Boon, an imprint of Harlequin (UK) Limited,
Large Print edition 2011
Eton House, 18-24 Paradise Road,
Richmond, Surrey TW9 1SR

© Marion Lennox 2011

ISBN: 978 0 263 22222 7

Harlequin (UK) policy is to use papers that are natural,
renewable and recyclable products and made from
wood grown in sustainable forests. The logging and
manufacturing process conform to the legal environmental
regulations of the country of origin.

Printed and bound in Great Britain
by CPI Antony Rowe, Chippenham, Wiltshire

With grateful thanks to Anne Gracie
and her Chloe, a matched pair of
great friends, to Trish Morey,
whose skill with words is awesome,
and to the Maytoners, because we rock.

To Buster Keaton,
who loved our family with all his small heart.

CHAPTER ONE

How many drop-dead gorgeous guys visited Banksia Bay's First Grade classroom? None. Ever. Now, when the heavens finally decreed it was time to right this long-term injustice—it would have to be a *Friday*.

Misty took her class of six-year-olds for swimming lessons before lunch every Friday. Even though swimming had finished an hour ago, her braid of damp chestnut curls still hung limply down her back. She smelled of chlorine. Her nose was shining.

Regardless, a Greek God was standing at her classroom door.

She looked and looked again.

Adonis. God of Desire and Manly Good Looks. Definitely.

Her visitor looked close to his mid-thirties. Nicely mature, she thought. Gorgeously mature. His long, rangy body matched a strongly boned face and almost sculpted good looks. He wore faded jeans and an open-necked shirt with rolled up sleeves. Looking closer—and she *was* looking closer—Misty could see muscles, beautifully delineated.

But…did Adonis have a six-year-old son?

For the man in her doorway was linked by hand to a child, and they matched. They both wore jeans and white shirts. Their black hair waved identically. Their coppery skin was the colour that no amount of fake tan could ever produce, and their identical green eyes looked capable of producing a smile to die for.

But only Adonis was smiling. He was squatting and saying to the child, 'This looks the right place. They're painting. Doesn't this look fun?'

Son-of-Adonis didn't look as if he agreed. He looked terrified.

And, with that, Misty gave herself a mental slap, hauled herself back from thinking about drop-dead gorgeous males and back to where she should be thinking—which was in schoolmarm mode.

'Can I help you?'

Frank, Banksia Bay School Principal, should have intercepted this pair, she thought. If this was a new student she'd have liked some warning.

There should be an empty place with the child's name on it, paints with paper waiting to be drawn on, the rest of the class primed to be kind.

'Are you Miss Lawrence?' Adonis asked. 'There's no one in the Principal's office and the woman down the hall said this is Grade One.'

She smiled her agreement, but directed her smile to Son-of-Adonis. 'Yes, it is, and yes, I am. I'm Misty Lawrence, the Grade One teacher.'

The child's hand tightened convulsively in his father's. This definitely wasn't a social visit, then; this was deathly important.

'I'm sorry we're messy, but we're in the middle of painting cows,' she told the little boy, keeping her smile on high beam. She was standing next to Natalie Scotter's table. Natalie was the most motherly six-year-old in Banksia Bay. 'Natalie, can you shift across so our visitors can see the cow you're painting?'

Natalie beamed and slid sideways. Misty could see what she was thinking. Hooray, excitement. And the way this guy was smiling…Misty felt exactly the same.

Um…focus. Get rid of this little boy's fear.

'Yesterday we went to see Strawberry the cow,' she told him. 'Strawberry belongs to Natalie's dad. She's really fat because she's about to have calves. See what Natalie's done.'

The little boy's terror lessened, just a little. He gazed nervously at Natalie's picture—at Natalie's awesomely pregnant cow.

'Is she really that fat?' he whispered.

'Fatter,' Natalie said, rising to the occasion with aplomb. 'My dad says it's twins and that means he'll have to stay up all night 'cos it's always a b…' She caught herself and gave Misty a guilty grin. 'I mean, sometimes he needs to call the vet and then he swears.' She beamed, proud of how she'd handled herself.

'Here's her picture,' Misty said, delving into the pocket of her overalls for a photograph. She glanced at Adonis, asking a silent question, and got a nod in response. This, then, was the way to go. 'Would you like to sit by Natalie and see if you can paint as well?' she asked. 'If it's okay with your dad.'

'Of course it is,' Adonis said.

'You can share my paints,' Natalie declared expansively, and Misty gave a tiny prayer of thankfulness that Natalie's current best friend was at home with a head cold.

'Thank you,' Son-of-Adonis whispered and

Misty warmed to him. He was polite as well as cute. If he *was* a new student…

'We're here to enrol Bailey for school,' Adonis said, and she smiled her pleasure, but she was also thinking, *Where is Frank?* And why did this pair have to arrive now when she felt like a chlorinated wet sheep?

'I know I should have made an appointment,' Adonis said, answering her unspoken question. 'But we only arrived in town an hour ago. The closer we got, the more nervous Bailey was, so we thought the sensible thing would be to show him that school's not a scary place. Otherwise, Bailey might get more nervous over the weekend.'

'What a good idea. It's not scary at all,' she said, warming to the man as well as to the son. 'We like new friends, don't we, girls and boys?'

'Yes.' It was a shout, and it made Misty smile. In this sequestered town, any newcomer was welcomed with open arms.

'Are you here for long?' she asked. 'You and your…family?' Was Mrs Adonis introducing another child to another class?

'There's only Bailey and me, and we're intending to live here,' he said, stooping to load Bailey's paintbrush with brown paint. Being helpful. But

Bailey checked Strawberry's photograph again, then looked at his father as if he'd missed the point. He dipped his brush in the water jar and went for red.

His father grinned and straightened, and held out his hand. 'I'm Nicholas Holt,' he said, and Misty found her hand enveloped in one much larger, much stronger. It was a truly excellent handshake. And his smile...

Manly Good Looks didn't begin to cut it, she thought. Wow! Forget Greek Gods. Adonis was promptly replaced with Nicholas.

She was absurdly aware of her braid, still dripping down her back. She wanted, quite suddenly, to kill Frank. It was his job to give warning of new parents. Why wasn't he in his office when he should be?

She didn't have so much as powder on her nose. It was freckled and it glowed; she knew it did. Her nose was one of the glowingest in the district. And five feet four inches was too short. Where were six inches when she needed them? If Frank had warned her, she might have worn heels.

Or maybe not.

'Miss...' a child called.

'I'm sorry; we shouldn't be disturbing your

class,' Nicholas said and she managed to retrieve her hand and force herself to think schoolteacherly thoughts. Or mostly schoolteacherly thoughts.

'If Bailey's to be my student, then you're not interrupting at all,' she said and turned to the child who'd called. 'Yes, Laurie, what do you need?'

'There's a dog, miss,' Laurie said from across the room, sounding agitated. 'He's bleeding.'

'A dog…' She turned to the window.

'He's under my table, miss, in the corner,' Laurie said, standing up and pointing. 'He came in with the man. He's bleeding everywhere.'

Help.

There were twenty-four children looking towards Laurie's table. Plus Nicholas Holt.

A bleeding dog…

There were kids here who'd make this up but Laurie wasn't one of them. He wasn't a child with imagination.

Laurie's table was in the far back corner, and the row of shelving behind it made for a small, dark recess. If a dog was under there…it couldn't be a very big dog.

'Then we need to investigate,' she said, as brightly as she could. 'Laurie, can you go and sit in my teacher's chair, please, while I see what's happening?'

Laurie was there like a shot—the best treat in the world was to be allowed to sit in his teacher's big rotating chair. With the way clear, Misty would be able to see…

Or not. She stooped, then knelt. It was dark under the table. Her hands met something wet on the floor—something warm.

Blood.

Her eyes grew accustomed to the gloom. Yes, there was a dog, cowering right back into the unused shelves.

She could see him clearly now, cringing as far back as he could get.

An injured dog could snap. She couldn't just pull him out.

'Can I help?'

He was Adonis. Hero material. Of course he'd help.

'We have an injured dog,' she said, telling the children as well as Ad…as well as Nicholas. 'He seems frightened. We all need to stay very quiet so we don't frighten him even more. Daisy, can you fetch me two towels from the swimming cupboard?'

'Do you know the dog?' Nicholas asked as Daisy importantly fetched towels. He was standing right over her, and then he was kneeling. His body was disconcertingly solid. Disconcertingly male.

He was peering underneath Laurie's table as if he had no idea in the world what his presence was doing to her.

What, exactly, was his presence doing to her?

Well, helping. That was a rarity all by itself. Misty was the fixer, the one who coped, the practical one. She did things by herself, from necessity rather than choice.

She didn't often have a large attractive male kneeling to help.

Often? Um…never.

'Do you know the dog?' he asked again and she got a grip on the situation. Sort of.

'No.'

'But he's injured?'

'There's blood on the floor. Once I have the towels, I can reach in…'

'It'll be safer if I lift the table so we can see what we're dealing with. Tell you what. If we move the kids back, it'll give him a clear run to the entrance. If he wants to bolt, then he can.'

'I need to see what's wrong.'

'But you don't want a child getting in the way of an injured animal.'

'No,' she said. Of course not.

'I left the outside door open from the porch,' he said. 'I'm sorry; that's how he must have come in. I can shut it now. That means if I lift the table and he bolts we have a neat little space to hold him.

She thought that through and approved. Yes. If the dog was scared he'd run the way he'd come. They could close the classroom door into the porch and they'd have him safe.

But to trap an injured dog…

This was NYP. Not Your Problem. That was what Frank would say. The School Principal was big on what was or wasn't his problem. He'd let the dog go, close the door after it and forget it.

But this wasn't Frank. It was Nicholas Holt and she just knew Nicholas wasn't a NYP sort of guy.

And in the end there wasn't a choice—the dog didn't give her one. She knelt, towels at the ready. Nicholas lifted the desk, but the dog didn't rush anywhere. The little creature simply shook and shook. He backed harder into the corner, as if trying to melt into the wall, and Misty's heart twisted.

'Oh, hush. Oh, sweetheart, it's okay, no one's going to hurt you.'

This little one wasn't thinking of snapping—he was well past it. She slipped the towels around him carefully, not covering his head, simply wrapping him so she could propel him forward without doing more damage.

He was a cocker spaniel, or mostly cocker spaniel. Maybe a bit smaller? He was black and white, with black floppy ears. He had huge black eyes. He was ragged, bloodstained and matted and there was the smell of tyre rubber around him. Had he been hit?

He had a blue collar around his neck, plastic, with a number engraved in black. She knew that collar.

A couple of years back, Gran's ancient beagle-cross had slipped his collar and headed off after a scent. Two days later, he'd turned up at the Animal Welfare Centre, with one of these tags around his neck.

This was an impounded dog. A stray.

No matter. All that mattered now was that the dog was in her arms, quivering with fear. There was a mass of fur missing from his hind quarters, as if he'd been dragged along the road, and his left hind leg looked…appalling. He was bleeding, sluggishly but steadily, and his frame was almost skeletal.

He needed help, urgently. She wanted to head out to her car right now and take him to the vet.

She had twenty-four first graders looking at her—and Nicholas was looking at her as well. NYP? She had problems in all directions.

'He's hurt.' It was a quavering query from Bailey. The little boy had sidled back to his father's side and slipped his hand in his. His voice was full of horror. 'Has he been shot?'

Shot? What sort of question was that?

'He looks like he's been hit by a car,' she said, to the class as well as to Bailey. Every first grader was riveted to the little animal's plight now. 'He's hurt his leg.' Anything else? She didn't know.

She looked down at him and he looked up at her, his eyes huge and pain-filled and hopeless. His shivering body pressed against hers, as if desperate for warmth.

She'd owned dogs since childhood. She loved dogs. She'd made a conscious decision not to have another one.

But this one… He was an injured stray and he was looking at her.

Uh oh.

'Do you want me to call someone to deal with him for you?' That was from Nicholas—with that question he surely wasn't Adonis. This wasn't a hero type of question. This the sort of response she'd expect from Frank.

Find someone to deal with him. Who?

Frank himself? If the Principal wasn't in his office, she had no one to turn to. Every other teacher had their own class.

She could make a fast call to Animal Welfare. This was their dog. Their problem. They'd collect him.

That was the sensible solution.

But the dog quivered against her, huddling tight, as if he was desperate for the poor amount of warmth she could provide. His eyes were pools of limpid despair.

He looked at her.

NYP. NYP.

Since when had anything ever been Not Her Problem? There was no way this dog was going back to one of the Welfare cages.

She did not need a dog. She did not!

But in her arms the dog quivered and huddled closer. She felt the silkiness of his ears. She could feel his heart, beating so fast… He was so afraid. He was totally at the mercy of the decision she made right now.

And, with that thought, her vow to leave dogs behind disintegrated to nothing.

What were dreams, anyway?

'Mr Holt, I need your help,' she said, attempting to sound like a teacher in control of the situation.

'Yes,' he said, sounding cautious. As well he might.

'I can't leave the children,' she said. 'This dog needs to go to the vet. That's what happens with sick dogs, doesn't it, boys and girls. You remember Dr Cray? We visited his surgery last month. I'm going to ask Bailey's father if he'll take him to Dr Cray for us. Will you do that for us, sir?'

Then she looked straight at Nicholas, meeting those deep green eyes head on. Not His Problem? Ha. He was asking her to teach his child. Payback happened early in Banksia Bay.

'I don't know about dogs,' he said, sounding stunned.

'That's okay,' she said, wrapping the little dog

more tightly in his towels. Before he could demur, she handed him over, simply pressing the dog against his chest and letting her hands fall. She wasn't about to drop him, but he wasn't to know that. He was forced to release Bailey to take the dog.

'Dr Cray does a midday surgery, so he should be there,' she said. Then, as he still looked flabbergasted, she thought maybe a little more explanation might be required. Explanation but no choice. She couldn't afford to give him a choice.

She so wanted to take this dog herself, but some things weren't possible. Nicholas would have to do.

'I'm not sure where our Principal is,' she said. 'These children are mostly country kids. We know about injured animals. We know the vet can help, only first we need to get him there. We ask our parents to help all the time—four of our mums and dads helped with swimming lessons this morning. I know Bailey's only just joined the class but we know you'll want to help as well. So please, can you take this dog to the vet? Tell Dr Cray I'll be there after work and I'll take care of the expenses.'

And she mustn't forget Bailey, she told herself.

She was asking a lot here—of both father and son.

She looked down at Bailey and something in his expression caught her. Made her remember…

Her mother, walking into her classroom on one of her fleeting visits. Misty might have been as old as Bailey, or maybe a little younger.

Her mother staying for all of two minutes—'just to see my kid'. Speaking gaily to her teacher as she walked out. 'You look after my Misty; she's such a good girl.' Then leaving. As she always left. Sending postcards from a life that didn't include Misty.

Whoa. In the midst of this drama, where had that thought come from? But the memory of it was there, in Bailey's eyes. She knew instinctively that his world wasn't certain, and she was asking more of him.

But, unfair or not, she had no choice. She couldn't leave the classroom and she could hardly toss the dog outside untended. What to do?

Give him the choice, as she'd never been given the choice.

She stooped. 'Bailey, we need your father's help to take this dog to where he can get bandages on his cut leg. Will you go with your dad to the vet's, or will you stay here with us and paint cows? Your dad will come back after he's left the dog with the vet. Won't you, sir? Is that okay with you, Bailey?'

Big breath. She was asking so much. And if she was right in what she sensed...if this little boy had been left in the past...

But it seemed Bailey trusted his father far more than she'd trusted her mother. He thought about it for a moment, looked up at the little dog wrapped in towels and then he gave a solemn nod, answering for both of them.

'My dad can take the dog to the vet.'

'That's wonderful.' It was indeed wonderful. 'Aren't dads great? Will you stay with us or will you go with him?'

'Stay with us,' Natalie said urgently, and Misty blessed Natalie's bossy little boots. 'I have heaps of paint.'

'I'll stay,' Bailey said, giving a cautious smile to Natalie.

'That's excellent.' She straightened and the look she gave Bailey's father was pure pleading. This was outrageous. If Frank could hear what she was doing he'd sack her on the spot. But what choice did she have?

'So will you do it for us?' she asked, and the dog looked hopelessly out at her from where it was cradled against his chest and she knew she was pleading for all of them. For the kids in her classroom, too. Every single one of them wanted a happy outcome for this dog.

'Please?'

CHAPTER TWO

WHAT had just happened?

One minute he had been a father intent on en-rolling his son in his new school. He'd been ready to fill in forms, reassure Bailey, do all the things a responsible dad did.

The next he was standing in the sunshine, his arms full of bleeding dog, with a worried school-teacher watching his rear. Making sure he fol-lowed directions.

An army commander couldn't have done it better.

Bailey would be safe with her.

That was a dumb thing to think at such a time—after all, what risk was there in leaving his son in a country primary school, in Australia, in a tiny seaside town where the most exciting thing to happen was…was…

Well, a dog being run over, for a start. Even that was more excitement than Nick wanted.

And it was a whole lot more excitement than

this dog wanted. As Nick felt the dog tremble he put the *me* angle aside and focused on the creature he was carrying.

There'd been no time to examine him in the classroom. Miss Lawrence had wanted him out of there.

That was unfair. Her first responsibility must be to the children in her class and she'd put them first. If she'd taken the time to see exactly what was wrong, then the children, too, would have seen. Maybe that would have been distressing.

So he did what he was told. He turned his back on the school and headed for the car.

To the vet?

That, at least, was easy. Banksia Bay's commercial centre consisted of the one High Street running down to the harbour. Right on the town's edge was a brick building set back from the road. There was a big tree out front, a large blue sign saying 'Vet' and a picture of a dog with a cocked leg, pointing to the tree.

He and Bailey had smiled at it when they'd arrived in town. It was barely a block and a half from the house he'd rented.

'We could get a dog,' Bailey had said, but tentatively because maybe he'd already known the answer.

The answer would be no. Nick wanted nothing else that would tear their hearts. He was totally responsible for Bailey now, and for Bailey to have any more tragedy...

Look at this dog, for instance—running away, being hit by a car. He didn't know how badly it was injured. In all probability, there was still a tragedy here.

If there was then he'd lie to Bailey, he decided. This dog obviously belonged to a nice farmer who lived a long way out of town. The farmer would come and collect him. No, it'd be too far to visit...

The dog in question quivered again in his arms—the trembling was coming in waves—and he stopped thinking of difficulties. The sensible thing would be to set the dog on the car seat beside him but when he went to put him down he shook so much he thought okay, if it's body warmth he needs, then why not give it to him?

If Miss Lawrence was here she'd hold him. She'd expect him to hold him too.

She was one bossy woman.

Strong? Independent? Like Isabelle?

Not like Isabelle. She was a country school-teacher. She wasn't a risk-taker.

She was...cute?

Now there was a dumb thing to think. He'd come here to set himself and Bailey up as safe and immune from any more risk—from any more tragedy.

From any more complications.

Isabelle had been dead for little more than a year. Even though their marriage had been on the rocks well before that, it hadn't made her death less shocking. Less gut-wrenching. It was far too soon to think that anyone, much less Bailey's new schoolteacher, was cute.

Hard not to think it, though. And maybe it was okay. Normal, even. She was a country school-teacher and her ability to intrude on his life would be limited to teaching his son.

And asking him to take a dog to the vet.

It took two minutes to drive the short distance to the vet's. When he carried the dog in, an elderly guy with heavy spectacles and a grizzled beard emerged from the swing doors behind Reception. His glance at Nick was only fleeting; he focused straight away on the blood-stained towel.

'What's happened?'

A man after my own heart, Nick thought. Straight to the core of the problem.

'Miss Lawrence from the local school asked me to bring this dog in,' he said as the vet folded back an edge of the towel so he could see what he was dealing with.

'Misty?' The vet was touching the dog's face, running his fingers down his neck. Feeling for his pulse. 'Misty doesn't have a dog.'

'No, he ran into the schoolroom while...'

But the vet had found the collar. He fingered the nylon—checked the number, winced.

'It's the second.'

'Sorry?'

'From our local Animal Welfare Centre.' The vet took the dog from him, holding him with practised ease. 'Henrietta gives dogs every chance, only there are never enough homes. When the dogs have stayed there for...well, it's supposed to be ten days but she stretches it as long as she has room...she brings them to me. Three months after Christmas, cute pups turn into unwanted dogs. Yesterday morning she had a van full and some driver ran into the back of her. Dogs went everywhere. This is one of them.'

'So...' Nick said, and paused.

'So,' the vet said heavily. 'Thank you for bringing him in.' He paused and then craggy eyebrows
raised. 'It's okay,' he said gently. 'I promise it'll
be painless.' And then, as Nick still hesitated,
'Unless you want a dog?'

'I…no.'

'You're not a local.' It was a statement.

'My son and I have just moved here.'

'Have you just? Got a house with a yard?'

'Yes, but…'

'Every kid needs a dog.' It was said neutrally,
probing a possible reprieve.

'No.' Yet still he hesitated.

'No pressure,' the vet said. 'The last thing this
guy needs is another place that doesn't want
him.'

'Miss Lawrence says she'll pay,' Nick said. 'For
you to treat him.'

'Misty said that?'

'Yes.'

'She wants to keep him?'

'I'm not sure.'

The vet seemed confused. 'Misty's dog died
last year. She's sworn she won't get another.'

'I'm sorry. I don't know any more than you
do.'

'She won't have realised he's due to be put

down. Or maybe she has.' The vet sighed. 'Trust Misty. Talk about a soft touch…' He glanced at his watch. Grimaced. 'I need to talk to her, but I won't be able to catch her until after school. That's almost three hours.' He looked at the dog again and Nick could see what he was thinking—that three hours was too long to make a dog suffer if the end was inevitable.

This wasn't Nick's problem. He should walk away. But…

But he had to face Misty, the bossy little school-teacher with the pleading eyes. Did she see this as her dog?

She'd said she'd cover the expenses. He had to give her the choice.

'I'm going back to the school anyway,' he said diffidently. 'I was enrolling my son when we found the dog. I could talk to her and phone you back.'

The vet's face cleared. 'Excellent. Let's do a fast assessment of this guy's condition so Misty knows what we're dealing with. She's not a girl to mess me around—it'll be yes or no. Can you give me a hand? I'll give him some pain relief and we'll tell her exactly what she is or isn't letting herself in for.'

* * *

Bailey drew a great cow. Misty gazed down at the child's drawing with something akin to awe. He was six years old, and his cow even looked like a cow.

'Wow,' she said as she stamped his picture with her gold elephant stamp—gold for Effort, elephant for Enormous. 'You must really like drawing, Bailey.'

'My dad can draw,' Bailey said. 'People pay him to draw pictures of boats.'

His father was an artist?

'Then you've come to the right place,' she said, glancing out of the window towards the distant harbour.

Nicholas Holt didn't look like an artist, she thought, but then, what did she know of artists? What did she know of anything beyond the confines of this town?

Don't think it. There was no point going down that road. For now, Banksia Bay was her life.

And for how much longer? She'd just offered to pay for a dog.

How long did dogs live?

'Story time,' she said determinedly. 'Tell you what, Bailey, as you're the new boy today, you can choose the story. Any book from the rack. Take a look.'

Bailey looked at her dubiously but he'd obviously decided this was an okay environment—this was somewhere to be trusted. And chubby little Natalie was right beside him, his new Friend For Life.

'Choose *Poky Little Puppy*,' Natalie whispered as only a six-year-old could whisper. "Cos it's all about a puppy getting into trouble, like your new dog.'

Like your new dog...

Uh oh.

'He's not Bailey's new dog,' Misty said as she settled on the reading stool with the kids around her.

'Then whose is he, miss?' Natalie asked, and she knew the answer. She'd known it as soon as she'd seen the plastic collar.

She sighed. She was stuck here anyway. Why keep fighting the odds? Her dreams had already stretched a lifetime and it seemed they needed to be stretched a while longer.

'I guess he's mine.'

* * *

And ten minutes later when Nick walked back into the classroom the thing was settled. He entered the room, Natalie's hand shot up and she asked before Misty could give permission.

'Please, sir, how's Miss Lawrence's dog?'

Miss Lawrence's dog. He flashed a look at Misty and she met his gaze with every evidence of serenity. As if she picked up stray dogs all the time.

Why? Dogs must give her heartache upon heartache, he thought. The lifespan for a dog was what? Sixteen years? The mutt in question was around ten years old already and battered, which meant he was sliding towards grief for all concerned. He had six years, at most—if he made it through the next twenty-four hours.

'He has a broken leg,' he said, aware of a classroom of eyes, but aware most acutely of Bailey. Bailey, who'd seen far too much horror already. Because of his father's stupidity…

'Is Dr Cray fixing him?' Misty asked from the front of the room, and his gaze locked on hers. He could reply without speaking; he knew this woman was intelligent enough to get it.

'It's an extremely expensive operation to fix his leg,' he said, trying for a neutral tone. 'He's already an elderly dog, so there may be complications. Apparently he's from the Animal Welfare Centre—a stray—but Dr Cray says he's willing to take care of him for us. All he needs is your permission. I can phone him now and let him know it's okay.'

She got the message. He saw her wince.

The vet was letting her off the hook. All she had to do was nod and go back to reading to the children. Nicholas would relay her decision and the problem would be solved.

But this woman didn't work like that. He sensed it already and her response was no surprise.

'How expensive?'

So she couldn't save the dog at any cost. She was a schoolteacher, after all.

What to say? He ran over the options fast.

Could they talk outside? Could he say, *Let's talk without the children hearing.* Let's give you the cold facts—that this dog's going to cost a mint; he's a stray with a limited lifespan. No one wants him; the kindest thing is to let Dr Cray do what he thinks best, which is to put him down.

He'd come to Banksia Bay to be sensible. He had to be sensible.

But then…Bailey was looking up at him with

huge eyes. Bailey would want details about what happened to the dog. Could he tell him the story about the distant farmer?

Could he lie?

All the children were looking at him. And their teacher?

Their teacher was looking trapped.

She had a dog.

The dog had trembled and cringed against her. He'd looked up at her, and she'd disappeared into those limpid eyes. His despair had twisted her heart.

But reality had now raised its ugly head and was staring her down.

How much was *extremely expensive*?

Becky, her best friend from school days, had just spent twelve thousand dollars on her Labrador's hip. But then, Becky had a property developer husband. Money was no problem. How badly was this dog's leg damaged?

Was she being totally stupid?

She thought of her wish list—twelve lovely things for her to dream about. To replace her list with a dog...

'I might not be able to aff...' But she faltered,

knowing already that she would afford—how could she not? The moment she'd seen those eyes she knew she was hooked.

But then, amazingly, Nick stopped her before she could say the unsayable.

'He's a stray,' he said gently. 'But if you're offering to keep him, then Bailey and I will pay for his operation. We left the school door open. It may even have been our fault that he was run over—maybe he saw the open door from across the street and ran here for shelter. You tell me that in Banksia Bay parents are asked to volunteer for jobs? This, then, is our job. If he's your dog, then we'll pay.'

Misty stared up at him, astounded. Her thoughts were whirling.

Extremely expensive was suddenly no cost at all.

No cost except putting her dreams on hold yet again.

How could she not?

Nicholas was looking at her. Her whole class was looking at her.

'Fine,' she said weakly. 'I do need a dog.'

Dreams were just that—dreams.

* * *

Frank arrived then, blustering away his absence, playing the School Principal to Nicholas and to Bailey. Misty used the time to excuse herself and phone Dr Cray to say she was accepting Nicholas's very kind offer.

'Misty, love, are you out of your mind?' the vet demanded. 'You need this dog like a hole in the head. He's old, neglected and he'll need ongoing treatment for the rest of his life.'

'He's got lovely eyes. His ears… He's a sweet-heart, I know he is.'

'You can't save them all. You swore you didn't want another dog. What about your list?'

'You know that's just a dream.'

Of course he did. This was Banksia Bay. The whole town knew everyone else's brand of tooth-paste. So the town knew about her list, and they'd know her chances of achieving it had just taken another nosedive.

She cringed, but she couldn't back down now. It'd be like tearing away a part of herself—the part that said, *Good old Misty; you can always depend on her.* The part where her heart was. 'I've fallen for him,' she said, softly but deter-minedly. 'Now that Mr Holt's paying…'

'And that's something else I don't understand. Who is this guy?'

'I don't know. A painter. New to the town.'

A pause. Then… 'A painter. I wonder how he'd go painting props.'

Fred Cray was head of Banksia Bay Repertory Society. There was a lot more to moving to Banksia Bay than just emptying a moving van. Did Nicholas realise it?

Maybe he already had.

'Give him a day or so before you ask,' she pleaded. 'Just save my dog.'

'You're sure?'

'Yes.'

So she had a dog again. At one time she'd been responsible for Gran, for Grandpa and for four dogs. Her heart had been stretched six ways. Now she was down to just Gran.

But who was wishing Gran away? She never would, and maybe taking this dog was simply accepting life as it was.

Banksia Bay. What more could a girl want?

New blood, at least, she thought, moving her thoughts determinedly to a future. With a dog.

And, with that, she decided she wouldn't mind a chance to get to know Nicholas Holt. She at least needed to thank him properly. But when she returned to the classroom Frank ushered Nicholas straight out to his office, and that was the last she saw of him for the day.

Bailey stayed happily until the end of school—any hint of early terror had dissipated in the face of Natalie's maternal care—and then Frank declared himself on gate duty, probably so he'd be seen by this new parent to be doing the right thing.

For there was something about Nicholas...

See, that was the problem. There was something about Nicholas Holt that made Frank think maybe he ought to stick around, be seen, just in case Nicholas turned out to be someone important.

He had the air of someone important.

A painter?

It didn't seem...right, Misty thought. He had an air of quiet authority, of strength. And he also had money. She knew now what the little dog's operation would cost and he hadn't hesitated. This was no struggling single dad.

She cleared up the classroom and headed out to find a deserted playground. What did she expect? That he'd stick around and wait for her?

He'd made one generous gesture and he'd moved

on. He had a house to move into. A future to organise.

Boats to paint?

She headed for the car and then to where she always went after school, every day without fail. Banksia Bay's nursing home.

Gran was in the same bed, in practically the same position she'd been in for years. One stroke had robbed her of movement. The last stroke had robbed her of almost everything else. Misty greeted her with a kiss and settled back and told her about her day.

Was it her imagination or could she sense approval? Gran would have rescued the little dog. She'd probably even have accepted money from a stranger to do it.

'It's not like I'm accepting welfare,' she told Gran. 'I mean, he's saving the dog—not paying me or anything. It's me who has to pay for the dog's ongoing care.'

Silence.

'So what shall we call him?'

More silence. Nothing new there. There'd been nothing but silence from Gran for years.

'What about Nicholas?' she asked. 'After the guy who saved him.'

But it didn't seem right. Nicholas seemed suddenly...singular. Taken.

'How about Ketchup, then?' she asked. 'On account of his broken leg. He'll spend the next few months ketching up.'

That was better. They both approved of that. She just knew Gran was smiling inside.

'Then I'd best go see how Ketchup's getting on,' she told her grandmother. 'He's with Dr Cray. I'm sorry it's a short visit tonight, but I'm a bit worried...'

She gave her grandmother's hand a squeeze. No response. There never was.

But dogs had been her grandmother's life. She'd like Ketchup, she thought, imagining herself bringing a recuperating Ketchup in to see her. Who knew what Gran could feel or sense or see, but maybe a dog on her bed would be good.

It had to be good for someone, Misty thought. Another dog...

Another love?

Who needed freedom, after all?

Nick and Bailey had the house sorted in remarkably short time, probably because they owned little more than the contents of their car. The house was only just suitable, Nick thought as they worked. Maybe it hadn't been such a good idea to rent via the Internet. The photographs he'd seen appeared to have been doctored. The doors and windows didn't quite seal. The advertised view to the sea was a view *towards* the sea—there'd been a failure to mention a fishermen's co-op in between. There were no curtains, bare light bulbs, sparse floor coverings.

But at least it was a base to start with. They could make it better, and if the town worked out they'd buy something of their own. 'It's like camping,' he told Bailey. 'We'll pretend we're explorers, living rough. All we need is a campfire in the backyard.'

Bailey gave him a polite smile. Right. But the school experience had made them both more optimistic about the future. They set up two camp beds in the front room, organised the rudiments of a kitchen so they could make breakfast, then meandered down to the harbour to buy fish and chips for tea.

They walked for a little afterwards, past the boats, through the main street, then somehow they ended up walking past the vet's.

Misty had just pulled up. She was about to go in.

He should stay clear, he thought. Paying for the dog was one thing, but he had no intention of getting personally involved.

But Bailey had already seen her. 'Miss Lawrence,' he called, and Misty waved. She smiled.

She smiled at Bailey, Nick told himself sharply, because a man had to do something to defend himself in the face of a smile like that.

He didn't have any intention of smiling back. Distance, he told himself harshly. He'd made that resolution. Stay clear of any complication at all. The only thing—the only one—who mattered was his son.

He'd messed things up so badly already. How many chances did a man have to make things right?

But Misty was still smiling. 'Hi,' she said. 'Are you here to see how Ketchup is?'

'Ketchup?' Bailey was beaming, and Nick thought back to the scared little boy of this morning and thought, *What a difference a day makes.* 'Is that what his name is?'

'Absolutely.'

'Why?'

'He's a hopalong. He'll spend his life ketching up.'

Bailey frowned, his serious little brow furrowing as he considered this from all angles. Then his face changed, lit from within as he got it. 'Ketchup,' he said and he giggled.

Nick had no intention of smiling, but somehow... This felt good, he thought. More. It felt great that Bailey giggled. Maybe he could afford to unbend a little.

'Great name,' he told her.

'He'll be a great dog,' Misty said.

'How is he?'

'He was still under anaesthesia last time I rang. Did you know his leg was broken in three places?'

'That's bad,' Bailey said, his giggle disappearing. 'When I got shot my arm was only broken in one place.'

Misty stilled. 'You were shot?'

'I'm better now,' Bailey said and tugged up his sleeve, revealing a long angry scar running from his wrist to his shoulder. 'I had plaster and bandages on for ages and it hurt a lot. Dad and I stayed at the hospital for ages and ages while

the doctors made my fingers wiggle again but
now I'm better. So we came here. Can we see
Ketchup?'

'Of course,' she said, but her voice had changed.
He could well imagine why. She'd have visions
of drug deals, underworld stuff, gangsters... For
a small boy to calmly say he'd been shot...

So maybe that was okay, he thought. Maybe
it'd make her step back and it suddenly seemed
important that she did step back.

Why did he think this woman might want to
get close?

What was he thinking? *He wanted her to think
he was a gangster?* What sort of future was he
building for his son? Maybe he needed to loosen
up.

'Now?' Bailey was asking.

Misty glanced at Nick. Okay, he didn't want
to be a gangster, and he had to allow Bailey to
form a relationship with his teacher. He nodded.
Reluctantly.

And, even if she was thinking he might be
carrying a sawn-off shotgun under his jacket, despite his curt, not particularly friendly nod, Misty
smiled down at his son and her face showed nothing but pleasure.

'Wow, wait until we tell Ketchup you've had a broken arm,' she said. 'You'll be able to compare wounds.' She took Bailey's hand and tugged open the screen door. 'Let's see how he's doing.'

And she didn't even care if he was a gangster, Nick thought, feeling ashamed. All she cared about was his son.

Ketchup had looked bad this morning but he looked a lot worse now. He lay on towels in an open cage. His hind quarters were shaved, splinted and bandaged. He had a soft collar around his neck, presumably to stop him chewing his bandages, but he wasn't about to chew any time soon. He looked deeply asleep. The tubes attached to his foreleg looked scary.

'I have him heavily sedated,' Dr Cray said. 'Pain relief as well as something to calm him down. He's been deeply traumatised.'

'Do we know anything about him?' Misty looked down at the wretched little dog and she felt the same heart twist she'd felt this morning. Yes, it was stupid, taking him on, but there was no way she could help herself. This dog had come through so much… He had to have a second chance.

'He was at the Shelter for two weeks,' Fred Cray said, glancing at his card. 'No one's enquired about him. Rolf Enwhistle found him and another dog prowling round his poultry pen but they weren't exactly a threat to the hens. This one rolled over and whimpered when Rolf went near. They were both starving—no collars. They looked like they'd been dumped in the bush and been doing it tough for weeks.'

'Oh, Ketchup,' Misty breathed. She looked back to Nick then, and she smiled at him. Doubts about the wisdom of keeping this dog had flown. How could she consider anything else? 'And you've saved him for me.'

'It's okay,' Nicholas said, sounding uncomfortable.

'Will he be your dog now?' Bailey asked.

'He certainly will,' she said, still smiling, though her eyes were misting. 'I have the world's biggest couch. Ketchup and I can watch television together every night. I wonder if he likes popcorn.'

'He's a lucky dog to have found you lot,' Fred said—but Bailey was suddenly distracted.

'We don't have a couch,' he said urgently to his father. 'We need one.'

'We'll buy a couch,' Nicholas said. 'On Monday.'

'Can we buy a couch big enough for dogs?'

'We'll buy a couch big enough for you and me.'

'Can Miss Lawrence and Ketchup come over and sit on our couch?'

'There won't be room.'

'Then we need to buy a bigger couch,' Bailey said firmly. 'For visitors.'

'I suspect Ketchup might want to stick around home for a while,' Misty said, seeing conflicting emotions on Nicholas's face and deciding he'd paid for Ketchup's vet's fees—the least she could do was take the pressure off. 'Ketchup needs to get used to having a home.'

'That's what Dad says we need to do,' Bailey said.

'I hear you're moving into Don Samuelson's old place,' Fred said neutrally. 'That's a bit of a barn. You could fit a fair few couches in there.'

'We don't have anything except two camp beds and a kitchen table,' Bailey said, suddenly desolate, using the same voice he used when he said he really, really needed a hamburger. 'Our new house is empty. It's horrid. We don't have pictures or anything.'

'Hey, then Misty's your girl,' the vet said, nudging Misty. 'Give 'em your spiel, Mist.'

'No, I...'

'She wanted to be an interior designer, our Misty,' the vet said before she could stop him. 'Sat the exams, got great marks, she was off and flying. Only then her gran had the first of her strokes. Misty stayed home, did teaching by correspondence and here she is, ten years later. But we all know she does a little interior decorating on the side. Part-time, of course. There's not enough interior decorating in Banksia Bay to keep a girl fed, eh, Mist? But if you're in Don Samuelson's place... There's a challenge. A man'd need a good interior designer there.'

'I'm a schoolteacher,' Misty said stiffly.

'But the man needs a couch.' Fred could be insistent when he wanted to be, and something had got into him now. 'New to town, money to spend and an empty house. It's not exactly appealing, that place, but Misty knows how to make a home.'

'You could come and see and tell us what to buy,' Bailey said, excited.

'Excellent idea. Why don't you do it straight away?' the vet said. He glanced down at the little dog and his eyes softened. Like Misty, Fred fell in love with them all. That Nick had appeared from nowhere with the wherewithal to pay...and that Misty had offered the dog a home...

Uh oh. Misty saw his train of thought and decided she needed to back off, fast. Fred Cray had been a friend of her Grandpa's. He was a lovely vet but he was also an interfering old busybody.

'I need to go home,' she said.

'You've visited your gran and you ate a hamburger at Eddie's half an hour ago,' Fred said, and she groaned inside. There was nothing the whole town didn't know in Banksia Bay. 'The little guy and his dad had fish and chips on the wharf, so they've eaten, too. So why don't you go by his place now and give him a few hints?'

'There's no rush,' Nicholas said, sounding trapped.

'Yes, there is. We need a couch.' Bailey was definite.

'See,' Fred said. 'There is a rush. Misty, I'm keeping this little guy overnight. Come back in the morning and we'll see how he is. Nine tomorrow?'

'Yes,' she said, feeling helpless. She turned to Nicholas. 'But there's no need...I'm not really an interior decorator.'

'Bailey and I could do with some advice,' he admitted, looking as bulldozed as she felt. 'Not just on what couch to buy but where to buy it. Plus a fridge and beds and a proper kitchen table. Oh, and curtains. We need curtains.'

'And a television,' Bailey said.

'You really have nothing?' Misty asked, astonished.

'I really have nothing. But I don't want to intrude...'

'You're not intruding. You're the answer to her dreams,' the vet said, chortling. 'A man with a blank canvas. Go with him, Misty, fast, before some other woman snaffles him.'

'I don't...' She could feel herself blush.

'To give him advice, I mean,' Fred said, grinning. 'You'll get that round here,' he told Nicholas. 'Advice, whether you ask for it or not. Like me advising you to use Misty. But that's good advice, sir. Take it or leave it, but our Misty's good, in more ways than one.'

CHAPTER THREE

PICK a quiet town in rural Australia, the safest place you can imagine to raise a child. Rent a neat house on a small block without any trees to climb and with fences all around. Organise your work so you can be a stay-at-home dad, so you can take care of your son from dawn to dusk. Hunker down and block out the world.

His plan did not include inviting a strange woman home on day one.

The vet had obviously embarrassed her half to death. She emerged from the clinic, laughing but half horrified.

'Fred's the world's worst busybody,' she said. 'You go home and choose your own couch.'

That was good advice—only Bailey's face fell.

If she was old and plain it'd be fine, he told himself, but her blush was incredibly cute and when she laughed she had this kind of dimple…

Danger signs for someone who wished to stay strictly isolated.

But maybe he was being dumb. Paranoid, even. Yes, she was as cute as a button, but in a girl-next-door way. She was Bailey's schoolteacher.

Maybe they needed a couch, he told himself, and found himself reassuring her that, yes, he would like some advice. There were so many decisions to be made and he didn't know where to start.

All of which was true, so he ushered her in the front door of their new home and watched her eyes light up with interest. Challenge. It was the way he felt when he had a blank sheet of paper and a yacht to design.

For Fred was right. This place was one giant canvas. They'd set up camp beds in the front room and slung a sheet over the windows for privacy. They had a camp table and a couple of stools in the kitchen. They'd picked up basic kitchen essentials.

They had not a lot else.

'You travel light,' she said, awed.

'Not any more, we don't.'

'We're staying here,' Bailey said, sounding scared again. The minute they'd walked in the door he'd grabbed his teddy from his camp bed and he was clutching it to him as if it were a lifeline. The house was big and echoey and empty. This was a huge deal for both of them.

Bailey had spent most of his short life on boats of one description or another, either on his father's classic clinker-built yacht or on his grandparents' more ostentatious cruiser. The last year or so had been spent in and out of hospital, then in a hospital apartment provided so Bailey could get the rehabilitation he needed. He had two points of stability—his father and his teddy. He needed more.

But where to start? To have a home…to own furniture… Nick needed help, so it was entirely sensible to ask advice of Bailey's schoolteacher.

He wasn't crossing personal boundaries at all.

'You really have nothing?' she asked.

'We've been living on boats.'

'Is that where Bailey was hurt?'

'Yes. It's also where Bailey's mother was killed,' he said briefly. She had to know that—as Bailey's teacher, there was no way he could keep it from her.

'I'm so sorry,' she said, sounding appalled.

'Yeah, well, we've come to a safer part of the

world now,' he said. 'All we need to make us happy is a couch.'

'And a dog?'

'No!'

'No?' she said, and she smiled.

She smiled ten seconds after he'd told her his wife had died. This wasn't the normal reaction. But then he realised Bailey was still within hearing. She'd put the appalled face away.

Bailey had had enough appalled women weeping on him to last a lifetime. This woman was smart enough not to join their ranks.

'A girl can always try,' she said, moving right on. 'Do you want all new stuff?'

'I don't mind.'

'Old stuff's more comfortable,' she said, standing in the doorway of the empty living room and considering. 'It'd look better, too. This isn't exactly a new house.' She stared around her, considering. 'You know, there are better houses to rent. This place is a bit draughty.'

'It'll do for now.' He didn't have the energy to go house-hunting yet. 'Do you have any old stuff in mind?'

She hesitated. 'You might not stay here for long.'

'We need to stay here until we're certain Banksia Bay works out.'

'Banksia Bay's a great place to live,' she said, but she was still looking at the house. 'You know, if you just wanted to borrow stuff until you've made up your mind, I have a homestead full of furniture. I could lend you what you need, which would give you space to gradually buy your own later. If you like, we could make this place home-like this weekend.'

'You have a homestead full of old stuff?'

'My place is practically two houses joined to-gether. My grandparents threw nothing out. I have dust covers over two living rooms and five bed-rooms. If you want, you can come out tomorrow morning to take a look.'

'Your grandparents are no longer there?'

'Grandpa died years ago and Gran's in a nursing home. There's only me and I'm trying to down-size. You're settling as I'm trying to get myself unsettled.'

He shouldn't ask. He shouldn't be interested. It wasn't in his new mantra—*focus only on Bailey*. But, despite his vow, she had him intrigued. 'By getting a new dog? That doesn't sound unsettled.'

'There is that,' she said, brightness fading a little. 'I can't help myself. But it'll sort itself out. Who knows? Ketchup might not like living with me. He might prefer a younger owner. If I could talk you into a really big couch...'

'No,' Nick said, seeing where she was heading.

'Worth a try,' she said and grinned and stooped to talk to Bailey. Bailey had been watching them with some anxiety, clutching his teddy like a talisman. 'Bailey, tomorrow I'm coming into town to pick up Ketchup. If I spend the morning settling him into his new home, would you and your dad like to come to my house in the afternoon to see if you can use some of my furniture?'

'Yes,' Bailey said. No hesitation. 'Teddy will come, too.'

'Excellent,' Misty said and rose. 'Teddy will be very welcome.' She smiled at Nick then. It was a truly excellent smile. It was a smile that could...

That couldn't. No.

'Straight through the town, three miles along the coast, the big white place with the huge veranda,' she was saying. 'You can't miss it. Any time after noon.'

'I'm not sure...'

'Oh, sorry.' Her face fell. 'You probably want all new furniture straight away. I got carried away. I'm very bossy.'

And at the look on her face—appalled at her assertiveness but still...hopeful?—he was lost.

Independence at all costs. He'd had enough emotion, enough commitment and drama to last a lifetime. There were reasons for his vows.

But this was his son's schoolteacher. She was someone who'd be a stalwart in their lives. He could be friendly without getting close, he told himself, and the idea of getting furniture fast, getting this place looking like home for Bailey, was hugely appealing.

And visiting Misty tomorrow afternoon? Seeing her smile again?

He could bear it, he thought. Just.

'We'll be extremely grateful,' he said, and Bailey smiled and then yawned, as big a yawn as he'd ever seen his son give.

'Bedtime,' he said, and Bailey looked through to the little camp bed and then looked at Misty and produced another of the smiles that had been far too rare in the last year.

'Can Miss Lawrence read me a bedtime story? She reads really good stories.'

'I'd love to,' Misty said, smiling back at him. 'If it's okay with your dad.'

It was okay, he conceded, but...

Uh oh.

There were all sorts of gaps in their lives right now, and this was only a small one, but suddenly it seemed important—and he didn't like to admit it. Not in front of a schoolteacher. In front of *this* schoolteacher.

'We don't have any story books,' he conceded.

What sort of an admission was that? He'd be hauled away to be disciplined by...who knew? Was there a Bad Parents Board in Banksia Bay? He felt about six inches tall.

They did own books, but they'd been put in storage in England until he was sure he was settled. Containers took months to arrive. Meanwhile...

'We'll buy some tomorrow,' he'd told Bailey.

'I have story books,' Misty said, seemingly unaware of his embarrassment.

'We've been living in a hospital apartment. Story books were provided.'

'You don't need to explain,' she said, cutting

through his discomfort. 'My car's loaded with school work—there'll be all sorts to choose from. If you would like me to read to Bailey...'

They both would.

Forget vows, he told himself. He watched Bailey's face and he felt the tension that he hadn't known he had ease from his shoulders.

For the last twelve months the responsibility for the care of his little son had been like a giant clamp around his heart. He'd failed him so dramatically... How could Bailey depend on him again?

Over the last year he'd been attempting to patch their lives back together and for most of that time he'd had professional help. But today they'd left behind the hospital and all it represented. This was day one of their new life together.

To admit that he needed help...to have Bailey want help and to have it offered... It should feel bad, but instead it made his world suddenly lighter; it made what lay ahead more bearable.

'We'd love you to read to Bailey,' he admitted, and it didn't even feel wrong.

'Then that's settled,' she said, beaming down at Bailey. 'I'm so glad you started school today. All weekend I'll know I have a new friend. Right, you get into your pyjamas and clean your teeth and I'll fetch a story book. I have my favourite in the car. It's about bears who live in a house just like this one, but every night they have adventures.'

'Ooh, yes, please,' Bailey said and the thing was settled.

So Nick sat on the front step, watched the sunset and listened to Misty telling his son a story about bears and adventures—and he found himself smiling. Unlike the bears, they'd come to the end of their adventures. The house was terrible but they could do something about it. This place was safe. This place could work.

He'd chosen Banksia Bay because it was a couple of hours drive to Sydney. It had a good harbour, a great boat building industry and it was quiet. He should have come and checked the house before he'd signed the lease but to leave Bailey for the four hours it'd take to get here and back, or explain what he was doing... He'd have had to come during office hours, and those hours he spent with his son.

Choosing this house was the price he'd paid, but even this wasn't so bad.

He couldn't see the sea from here but he could

hear it. That was good. To be totally out of touch with the ocean would be unthinkable.

He'd set up his office over the weekend. On Monday Bailey would start regular school hours. He'd be able to get back to work.

Work the new way.

The bear story was drawing to its dramatic conclusion. He glanced in the open window and Bailey's eyes were almost shut.

He'd sleep well in his new home—because of this woman.

She was so not his type of woman, he thought. She was a country mouse.

No. That was unjust and uncalled for. He accepted she was intelligent and she was kind. But her jeans were faded and her clothes were unpretentious. Her braid was now a ponytail. She'd changed since she'd cradled the dog this morning. She'd lost the bloodstains, but she must have changed at school because this shirt had paint on it already.

She was stooping now to give his son a kiss goodnight, and her ponytail looked sort of... perky? Actually, it was more sexy than perky, he thought, and he was aware of a stab of something as unexpected as it was unwanted.

The thought of those curls… He'd like to run his fingers through…

Whoa. How to complicate a life, he thought— have an affair with the local schoolteacher. He had no intention of having an affair with anyone. Let's just keep the hormones out of this, he told himself savagely, so when Misty came outside he thanked her with just a touch too much formality.

And he saw her stiffen. Withdraw. She'd got his unspoken message, and more.

'I'm sorry. I should have given you the book and left. I didn't mean to intrude.'

She was smart. She'd picked up on signals when he'd hardly sent them.

'You didn't intrude,' he said, and this time he went the other way—he put more warmth into his tone than he intended. He gripped her hand, and that was a mistake. The warmth…

How long since he'd touched a woman?

And there was another dumb thought. He'd been shaking hands with nurses, doctors, therapists every day. Why was Misty different?

He couldn't permit her to be different.

'You want to tell me about Bailey?' she asked and he did the withdrawal thing again. Released her hand, fast.

'It's on his medical form at school.'

'Of course it is,' she said, backing off again. 'I left school in a hurry because I wanted to get to the vet's, so I haven't caught up with the forms yet. I'll read them on Monday.' She turned away, heading out of his life.

She'd see the forms on Monday...

Of course she would, he thought, and he'd been frank in what he'd written. He'd had no choice. There were a thousand ways that keeping what happened to Bailey from his classroom teacher could cause problems. *Okay, boys and girls, let's pretend to be pirates...*

She had to know, and to force her to read the forms on Monday rather than telling her now... What was he trying to prove?

'I can tell you now,' he said.

He was all over the place.

He felt all over the place.

'There's no need...'

'There is a need.'

Why did it feel as if he were stepping on egg-shells? This was Bailey's teacher. Treat her as such, he told himself harshly. Treat her professionally, with cool acceptance and with an admission that she needed to know things he'd rather not talk about.

'I'm not handling this well,' he admitted. 'Today's been stressful. In truth, the last year's been stressful. Or maybe that's an understatement. The last year's been appalling.' He paused then, wanting to retreat, but he had to say it.

'I don't want to interrupt your evening any more than I already have, but if you have the time... You're Bailey's teacher. You need to know what he's been through.'

'I guess I do,' she said equably. 'We both want what's best for Bailey.'

That was good. It took the personal out of it. He was telling her—for Bailey.

He paused then and looked at her. She was a woman without guile, his kid's teacher. She was standing on the veranda of the home he was preparing for his son. She was a warm, comforting presence. Sensible. Solid. *Safe.*

His parents would approve of her, he thought, and the idea sent a wave of emotion running through him so strongly that he felt ill. If he'd chosen a woman like this rather than Isabelle...

Someone safe.

Someone he could trust if he let his guard down.

When had he last let his guard down?

'So tell me, then,' she said—and he did.

There was no reason not to.

It took a while to start. Nick fetched lemonade. He said he'd rather be drinking beer but he hadn't yet made it further than the supermarket. He apologised for there being no food but cornflakes. She said she didn't need beer and she wasn't hungry. She waited.

It was as if he had to find his mindset, as well as his place on the veranda.

Nick didn't look like a man who spent a lot of time in an easy chair, Misty thought, and when he finally leaned his rangy frame on the veranda rail she wasn't surprised. She was sitting on the veranda steps. The width of Bailey's window was between them. Maybe that was deliberate.

For a while he didn't say anything, but she was content to wait. She'd been teaching kids for years. Parents often needed to tell her things about their children; about their families. A lot of it wasn't easy. But what Nick had to say...

'Bailey's mother was shot off the coast of

Africa,' he said at last, and the words were such a shock she almost dropped her lemonade.

No one ever got shot in Banksia Bay. And...*off the coast of Africa?*

If this was one of her students, she'd give them a sheet of art paper and say, 'Paint it for me.' Dreams needed expression.

But one look at this man's face told her this was no dream. It might not happen in her world, but it did happen.

'She was killed instantly,' he said, and he was no longer looking at her. He was staring out at the blank wall of the fisherman's co-op, but she knew he was seeing somewhere far off. Somewhere dreadful. 'Bailey was shot as well,' he told her. 'It's taken almost a year to get him this far. To see him safe.'

What to say after a statement like that? She tried not to blurt out a hundred questions, but she couldn't think of the first one.

'It's a grim story,' he said at last. 'Stupidity at its finest. I've needed to tell so many people over the last year, but telling never gets easier.'

'You're not compelled to tell me.'

'You're Bailey's teacher. You need to know.'

'There is that,' she said cautiously. If she didn't

know a child's history, it was like walking through a minefield. 'Oh, Nicholas…'

'Nick,' he said savagely, as if the name was important.

'Nick,' she said—and waited. 'It's okay,' she said gently. 'Just tell me as much as I need to know.'

He shrugged at that, a derisory gesture, half mocking. 'Right. As much as you need to know. I was working on a contract in South Africa, Bailey and Isabelle were with Isabelle's parents. They were on a boat coming to meet me, they were robbed and Isabelle and Bailey were shot.'

'Oh, Nick…'

His face stopped her going any further. There was such emptiness.

'What's not obvious in that version is my stupidity,' he said, and she sensed that she was about to get a story that he hadn't told over and over. He no longer seemed to be talking to her. He seemed somewhere in his head, hating himself, feeding his hatred.

The hatred made her feel ill. She wanted to stop him, but there was no way she could.

If this man needed to talk, ugly or not, maybe she had to listen.

'As a kid I was…overprotected,' he said at last into the silence, and the impression that he wasn't talking to her grew stronger. 'Only child. Protected at every turn. So I rebelled. I did the modern day equivalent of running away to sea. I studied marine architecture. I designed boats, won prizes, made serious money. I built a series of experimental boats, and I took risks.'

'Good for you,' she murmured. Then she added, before she could help herself, 'Half your luck.'

'No,' he said flatly. 'Risks are stupid.'

'It depends on the risks,' she said, and thought of how many risks she'd ever encountered. Approximately none.

But then…this wasn't about her, she reminded herself sharply. Listen.

'My kind of risks were definitely the stupid kind,' he said and, despite her interjection, she still had the impression he was talking to himself. 'Black run skiing, ocean racing in boats built for speed rather than safety, scuba-diving, underwater caving… Fantastic stuff, but the more dangerous the better. And then I met Isabelle. She was like me but more so. Risks were like breathing to her. The stuff we did… Her parents were wealthy so she could indulge any whim, and Isabelle surely had whims. In time, I learned she was a little bit crazy. If I skied the hardest runs, she didn't ski runs at all. She skied into the unknown. Together, we did crazy stuff.'

'But you had fun?' She was trying to keep the wistfulness from her voice, not sure if she was succeeding. Nick glanced at her as if he'd forgotten she was there, but he managed a wry nod.

'We did. We built *Mahelkee*, our gorgeous yacht, and we sailed everywhere. I designed as I went. We had an amazing life. And then we had Bailey, and that was the most amazing thing of all. Our son.'

He hesitated then, and she saw where memories of good times ended and the pain began. 'But when I held him…' he said softly, 'for the first time I could see where my parents were coming from. Not as much, of course, but a bit.'

'So no black ski runs for Bailey?'

He was back staring at the side of the co-op. No longer talking to her. 'There were no ski runs where we lived but there was no way Isabelle was living in a house. We kept living on the boat. It caused conflict between us but we kept travelling. We kept doing stuff we loved. Only…when I saw the risky stuff I thought of Bailey. We started being careful.'

'Sensible.'

'Isabelle didn't see it like that.'

Silence.

This wasn't her business, she thought; she also wasn't sure whether he'd continue. She wasn't sure she wanted him to continue.

'You want to finish this another day?' she ventured, and he shook his head, still not looking at her.

'Not much more to tell, really. I'd married a risk-taker, and Isabelle was never going to change. Bailey and I just held her back. We were in England when I got a contract to design a new yacht. She was to be built in South Africa. I needed to consult with the builders.'

'So you went.'

'We were docked at a pretty English port. Isabelle's parents own the world's most ostentatious cruiser and they were docked nearby. Isabelle was taking flying lessons and they were keeping her happy. Everyone seemed settled; we were even talking about enrolling Bailey in kindergarten. So I flew across to South Africa. But Isabelle was never settled for long. She got bored with her flying lessons and persuaded her parents to bring their boat out to surprise me.'

'To Africa?'

'In a boat that screamed money.' There was no mistaking the bitterness in his voice now. The pain. 'To one of the poorest places on the planet. When I found out they were on their way I was appalled. I knew the risks. I had security people give them advice. I sent people out to meet them, only they were hit before they arrived.'

'Hit?'

He shrugged. 'What do you expect? Poverty everywhere, then along comes a boat with a swimming pool, crew in uniform, dollar signs practically painted on the sides. But they'd had good advice. If you're robbed, once you're boarded, just hand over everything. Isabelle's father carried so much cash it'd make your head swim. He thought he could buy himself out of any trouble. Maybe he could, but Isabelle…she decided to defend,' he said savagely.

Misty knew she didn't exist for him right now. There was no disguising the loathing in his voice and it was directed only at himself. 'I knew she owned a gun before we were married, but she told me she'd got rid of it. And I believed her. Of all the stupid…' He shook his head as if trying to clear a nightmare but there was no way he could clear what he was going through. 'So, as her father tried to negotiate, she came up from below deck, firing. At men who made their living from piracy. Two shots—that's all it took. Two shots and she was dead and Bailey was close to it.'

She closed her eyes, appalled. 'So that's why you're here,' she whispered.

'That's why we're here. Bailey's spent a year in and out of hospital while I've researched the safest place in the world to be. I can design boats from here. Most of my designs are built internationally. I've hired an off-sider who can do the travelling for me. I can be a stay-at-home dad. I can keep Bailey safe.'

'You'll wrap him in cotton wool?' She felt suddenly, dreadfully anxious. 'Small risks can be exciting,' she ventured. 'I can make my bike stand on its front wheel. That's meant the odd bruise and graze. There's risks and risks.'

'I will not take risks with my son's life.'

The pain behind that statement… It was almost over-whelming.

What to do?

Nothing.

'No one's asking you to,' she said, deciding brisk and practical was the way to go. 'You have a house to organise, a child to care for and boats to design. Our vet, Fred, has plans for your painting, and I might even persuade you to get a dog. You can settle down and live happily ever after. But if you'd never had those adventures...'

What was she talking about? Don't go there, she told herself, confused at where her mind was taking her. If he'd never had those adventures... like she hadn't?

This was not about her.

She made herself step down from the veranda. This man's life, his past, was nothing to do with her. She needed to return to the nursing home to make sure Gran was settled for the night. She needed to go home.

Home... The home she'd never left.

Nick didn't stop her. He'd withdrawn again, into his isolation, where risks weren't allowed. He seemed as if he was hardly seeing her. 'Thank you for listening,' he said formally.

'You're welcome,' she said, just as formally, and she turned and left before she could ask him—totally inappropriately—to tell her about Africa.

* * *

What was he about, telling a total stranger the story of his life? It was so out of character he felt he'd shed a skin—and not in a good way. He felt stupid and naive and exposed.

He'd never done personal. Even with Isabelle... He'd hardly talked to her about his closeted childhood.

So why let it all out tonight? *To his son's schoolteacher?*

Maybe it was because that was all she was, he decided. Bailey's teacher. Someone whose focus was purely on his son. Someone prepared to listen when he needed to let it all out.

Why let it out tonight?

Justification?

He stared around at the shabby house, the empty walls, the lack of anything as basic as a storybook, and he thought that was where it had come from. A need to justify himself in the eyes of Misty Lawrence.

Why did he need to justify himself?

He didn't want her to judge him.

That was stupid, all by itself. She was a country hick schoolteacher. Her opinion didn't matter at all.

If it did... If it did, then it'd come under the

category of taking risks, and Nicholas Holt no longer took risks.

Ever.

She went home, to her big house, where there was only herself and the sound of the sea.

Africa.

She'd just got herself a dog.

Africa.

Nick's story should have appalled her. It did.

But Africa…

Since Gran's stroke, she'd started keeping her scrapbooks in the kitchen where recipes were supposed to be. Dreams instead of recipes? It worked for her. She tugged the books down now and set them on the kitchen table.

She had almost half a book on Africa. Pictures of safaris. Lying at dawn in a hide, watching a pride of lions. The markets of Marrakesh.

Africa was number eight on her list.

She had a new dog. How long would Ketchup live?

She picked up a second scrapbook and it fell open at the Scottish Highlands. She'd pasted in a picture of a girl in a floaty white dress lying in a field of purple heather. Behind her was a mass of purple mountains.

She'd pasted this page when she was twelve. She'd put a bagpiper in the background, and a castle. Later, she'd moved to finer details. Somewhere she'd seen a documentary on snow buntings and they had her entranced—small birds with their snow-white chests and rippling whistle. Tiny travellers. Exquisite.

Birds who travelled where she never could. She had pictures of snow buntings now, superimposed on her castle.

She flicked on, through her childhood dreams. Another scrapbook. The Greek islands. Whitewashed houses clinging to cliff faces, sapphire seas, caiques, fishermen at dawn...

These scrapbooks represented a lifetime of dreaming. The older she was, the more organised she'd become, going through and through, figuring what she might be able to afford, what was feasible.

She'd divided the books, the cuttings, into months. She now had a list of twelve.

Exploring the north of England, the Yorkshire Dales, a train journey up through Scotland, Skara

Brae, the Orkneys…Bagpipers in the mist. Snow buntings. Number ten.

Greece. Number two.

Africa.

Risks.

Bailey.

She closed the book with a snap. Nicholas was right. You didn't take risks. You stayed safe.

She'd just agreed to keep another dog. She had no choice.

Her computer was on the bench. On impulse, she typed in *Nicholas Holt, Marine Architect* and waited for it to load.

And then gasped.

The man had his own Online Encyclopaedia entry. His website was amazing. There were boats and boats, each more wonderful than the last. Each designed by Nicholas Holt.

This man was seriously famous.

And seriously rich? You didn't get to design boats like these without having money.

That a man like this could decide Banksia Bay was the right place to be…a safe place to be…

'It makes sense,' she told herself, and she flicked off the Internet before she could do what she wanted to do—which was to research a little more about Africa.

'I have a dog now,' she told herself. 'Black runs are probably cold and wet. Doesn't Scotland have fog and midges? Who knows what risks are out there? So gird your loins, accept that dreams belong in childhood and do what Nick Holt has done. Decide Banksia Bay is the best place in the world.'

But dreams didn't disintegrate on demand.

Dogs don't live for ever, she told herself. Her list money was still intact. She could hold onto her dream a while longer.

One day she'd complete her list. In her retirement?

Maybe.

Just not one day soon.

CHAPTER FOUR

KETCHUP decided to live.

At nine the next morning Misty was gazing down at the little dog with something akin to awe. He was still hooked up to drips. His back leg was splinted and bandaged. He had cuts and grazes everywhere, made more gruesome by the truly horrid-coloured antiseptic wash, but he was looking up at her with his huge black eyes and... his tail was wagging.

It had lost half its fur and it had probably been a pretty scrappy tail to start with, but it was definitely wagging. The eyes that looked at her were huge with hope, and she fell in love all over again.

'How can he have been at the shelter for two weeks and no one claimed him?' she demanded of Fred, and the old vet smiled, took out the drips, bundled the little dog up and handed him over.

'Not everyone has a heart as big as yours,

Misty. Not everyone accepts responsibilities like you do.'

'What's one more responsibility?' she said and, yes, she felt a little bitter but, as she carried Ketchup out to her car, she wondered how she could feel bad about giving this dog a home.

There was no way she could leave Banksia Bay with Gran like she was. Ketchup would make life better—not worse.

She settled him onto the passenger seat and she talked to him the whole way home.

'You're going to like it with me. I have a great house. It's old and comfy and close to the beach, where you'll be able to run and run as soon as your leg's better. And there's so many interesting smells...' Then she couldn't stop herself adding a bit more exciting stuff because, for some reason, it was front and centre. 'And this afternoon we have two friends coming out to visit. Bailey and Nick. Nick's the one who saved you.'

He really had saved him. Fred had given her the facts.

'He's left his credit card imprint. Every cost associated with this dog, long-term, goes to Mr Holt. There's nothing for you to take care of. Yeah, he'll need ongoing care, but it's sorted.'

'He's a real hero,' she said, thinking of the website, of Nick's image, and of Nicholas last night. His care of his little son. His willingness to pay for Ketchup. The fact that he was haunted by his perceived failure to protect Bailey.

He was in such pain…

Ketchup wriggled forward and put his nose on her knee. Yes, he should be in a crate in the back but she figured this guy had had enough of crates to last a lifetime.

She was still thinking of Nick.

'He's our hero,' she told him. 'He's come to Banksia Bay to be safe, not heroic, but he's saved you. So maybe there's a little bit of hero left in him.'

A little bit of Adonis?

No. He was done with adventure. He was done with risk-taking.

He wanted to settle in Banksia Bay and live happily ever after.

Maybe even marry the local schoolteacher?

Where had that idea come from? A guy like that… She felt herself blush from the toes up.

But you need to settle as well, she told herself as she took her dog home. You have a great life here. A comfortable existence. All you need is a hero to settle with.

And put another rocker on the front porch so you can rock into old age together? I don't think so.

So what is it you want? she asked herself, and she knew the answer.

Life.

'Life's here,' she told herself out loud. 'Life's Banksia Bay and a new dog and a new pupil in my class. Woohoo.'

Ketchup pawed her knee and she felt the familiar stab of guilt.

'Sorry,' she told him. 'I love it here. Of course I do. I'd never do anything to upset you or Gran or anyone else in this place. You can come home and be safe with me.'

Safe with Misty.

A flash of remembered pain shafted through her thoughts. Her grandfather's first heart attack. Her grandmother, crippled with arthritis, terrified. Misty had been thirteen, already starting to understand how much lay on her shoulders.

And then her hippy mother had turned up, as unexpectedly and as briefly as she'd turned up less than half a dozen times in Misty's life. Misty remembered standing beside her grandfather's bedside, watching her grandmother's face drawn in fear. She remembered the mother she barely recognised hugging her grandmother, then backing out, to friends who never introduced themselves, to a psychedelic combi-van waiting to take her to who knew where? To one of the places the postcards came from.

'You'll be fine,' her mother had said to her grandmother, and she'd waved inappropriately gaily. 'I'm glad I could fit this visit in. I know Dadda will be okay. He's strong as a horse, and I know you'll both be safe with Misty.'

'See,' she told the little dog. 'My mother was right all along.'

There was no way he could miss Misty's house. It was three miles out of town, set well back from the road. There were paddocks all round it, undulating pastures with cattle grazing peacefully in the midday sun. The sea was its glittering backdrop, and Nick, who'd been to some of the most beautiful places on the earth, felt that this was one of them.

Here was a sanctuary, he thought. A place for a man to come home to.

Misty was on the veranda, easy to spot as they pulled up. She was curled up on a vast cane rocker surrounded by faded cushions. There was a rug over her knee.

Ketchup was somewhere under that rug. As they climbed from the car, Nick could see his nose.

Once again, that pang. Of what? Want? Of the thought that here was home? This place...

This woman.

He'd bared his soul to this woman last night. It should feel bad. Somehow, though, it didn't feel threatening.

'I can't get up,' she called, her voice lilting in a way he was coming to recognize, beginning to like. 'We've just gone to sleep.'

As if in denial, a tail emerged and gave a sleepy wag.

Bailey scooted up the steps to meet her, but Nick took his time, watching his son check the dog, smile at Misty, then clamber up onto the rocker to join them.

Something was happening in his chest.

This was like a scene out of *Little House on the Prairie*, he told himself, at the same time telling the lump in his throat to go down and stay down. The way he was feeling was kitsch. Corny.

Any minute now, Misty would invite them inside for home-baked cookies and lemonade. Or maybe she'd have a picnic to take down to the beach. She'd have prepared it lovingly beforehand, with freshly baked cakes, fragrant pies, home-made preserves. They'd be packed in a cute wicker basket with a red gingham cover…

'It's about time you got here,' she called, interrupting his domestic vision. 'I'm stuck.'

'Stuck?'

'I've been aching for lunch but Ketchup gets shivery every time I put him down. So I'm hoping I can stay here while you make me a sandwich.' She peeped up at him—cheeky. 'Cheese and tomato?'

'I could do that,' he said, waving goodbye to schmaltz and deciding cheeky was better. Much better.

'The bread's on the kitchen table. Cheese is in the fridge and tomatoes are out the back in the veggie garden. I like my cheese thick.'

Mama in *Little House on the Prairie* would never demand her man make a sandwich, Nick thought, and he grinned. Misty saw it.

'What?'

'I was expecting the table to be laid, Dresden china and all.'

'I have Dresden china,' she said, waving an airy hand. 'It's in the sideboard in the dining room. You're right, Ketchup and I would like our sandwich on Dresden china.'

'You're kidding.'

'Why would we kid about sandwiches on Dresden china?' She was helping Bailey snuggle down beside her. 'Important things, sandwiches. Would you like a sandwich, Bailey?'

'We've had lunch,' Bailey said shyly.

'Since when did that make a difference?' she asked, astonished. 'It's not a school day. We can eat sandwiches all afternoon if we want. Will we ask your daddy to make you a sandwich as well? Is he a good cook?'

'He cooks good spaghetti.'

'Not sandwiches?'

'I can make sandwiches,' Nick said, offended.

'Wonderful.' She beamed. 'Bailey, what sort of sandwich would you like?'

'Honey.' That was definite.

'We have honey. Can I add that to our order?' Misty asked and smiled happily up at Nick. 'Please?'

* * *

So he made sandwiches in Misty's farmhouse kitchen overlooking the sea, while Bailey and Misty chatted just outside the window.

He felt as if he'd been transported into another universe. He was making sandwiches while Bailey and Misty admired Ketchup's progress and compared Ketchup's bandaged leg to Bailey's ex-bandaged arm.

'My dad drew pictures on my plaster cast. Of boats.'

'Ketchup's more into bones. We'll ask him to draw bones on Ketchup's bandages.'

Bailey was giggling. *Giggling.*

This was too good to be true. His son was giggling on the veranda of a woman who was a part of his future.

His future?

Surely he meant Bailey's future. Misty was Bailey's teacher.

But his treacherous mind said *his* future.

He stabbed the butter and lifted a chunk on his knife, considering it with care. Where to take this?

This did not fit in with his plans.

He'd come to this place with a clear path in view. A steady future. Nothing to rock the boat.

Misty wouldn't mess with that.

So maybe he could just…see. He could let his barriers down a little. He'd let them down last night and there was no issue.

There were no risks down this road.

'Are you planning to hoist that butter on a flag-pole or put it on our bread?' Misty called through the window and he saw what he'd been doing and chuckled—and that in itself was amazing. When was the last time he'd felt like chuckling?

He made his sandwiches. He carried them outside, plus a bottle of not home-made lemonade, and he watched as Misty and Bailey munched and Ketchup woke a little and accepted a quarter of a sandwich and retired again.

'This is the best place for a dog,' Nick said. He'd settled himself on the veranda steps, not bothering so much about distance now but thinking more of view. If he leaned back at the top of the stairs he got a full view—of Misty.

And of Bailey and Ketchup, he reminded himself, but he was forgetting to remind himself so often,

'It's the best place for anyone,' Bailey declared. He'd eaten two more sandwiches on top of his lunch. For a child who'd needed to be coaxed to eat for a year, this was another thing to be amazed at.

Teddy, Nick noticed, had been set aside.

'It's pretty nice,' Misty said, but suddenly her voice sounded strained.

'Don't you like it?' Bailey asked.

'Yes.' But she didn't sound sure.

'Where else would you like to live?' Nick asked.

'In a yurt.'

He and Bailey both stared. 'A yurt?'

'Yep.'

'What's a yurt?' Bailey asked.

'My mother sent me a postcard of one once. It's a portable house. It's round and cosy and it packs up so I can put it on the back of my camel. Or my yak.'

Bailey was intrigued. 'What's a yak?'

'It's a sort of horse. Or maybe it's more like a sheep but it carries things. The yurt on my post-card had a camel in the foreground but I've been reading that camels bite. And yaks seem to be more common in Kazakhstan,' she said. 'That's where yurts are found. Probably in lots of other places, too, but I've never been there to find out. Yaks seem pretty friendly, or at least I think they are. I've never met one, but some day I will. That's my dream. Me and my yak will take our yurt and head into the unknown.'

'In term vacations?' Nick asked before he could help himself. Bailey did not need his new-found teacher to be heading off into the unknown.

'I'd need more than term vacation,' she retorted. 'To follow the dreams I have…' The lightness in her voice faded a little and she gave a wry smile. 'But of course you're right. Term vacations aren't long enough. It's only a dream.'

'And you have a really nice house,' Bailey said placatingly. 'It's big and comfy.' Then he looked at Misty's face and maybe he could see something there that Nick was sensing—something that was messing with his domestic harmony as well. 'Could you buy a little yurt and put it in the backyard?' he asked. 'Like a tent?'

'Maybe I could.' The lightness returned but it was determined lightness. 'Maybe I could buy a yurt on the Internet—or maybe we could build one as a school project.'

Bailey's eyes widened with interest. 'My dad could help you build one. He's good at building.'

'Could he?' Misty smiled, but Nick saw a wash of emotions put aside and thought there were things here he didn't understand. But then... Why should he want to understand this woman?

He did. There was something about her... Something...

'Can you, Dad?' Bailey asked.

'I'm not sure...' he started.

'Well, I am,' Misty declared. She tossed off her blankets in decision. 'I think Ketchup needs to stand on the grass for a bit and then we need to re-member why you came. We need to look at spare beds—I counted them last night and we have ten. Then I'm going to make a list of everything else you need in your house while you and your dad draw me a picture of a little yurt we could build in the school yard.' She rose and hugged her little dog tight against her. 'A little yurt would be fun and we can do without yaks. We don't need any-thing but what's in Banksia Bay, and why would a woman want anything but what's right here?'

They searched the Internet and learned about yurts. They drew more and more extravagant plans and then Nick got serious and sat down and designed one they really might be able to construct in the school yard. Then they explored the muddle of furniture in the largely unused house.

Misty was right—the place was huge. It had been a big house to start with, and she told him her great-grandparents had built an extension when her grandparents married. She had two kitchens and three living rooms. She owned enough furniture to cater for a small army, and she was offering him whatever he liked.

With Bailey's approval, Nick chose two beds, two couches, a table and chairs. He chose wardrobes, sideboards, armchairs. So much…

'Why don't you want it?' Bailey asked, intrigued.

'There's only me,' Misty said. 'And Ketchup,' she added. She was carrying the dog along with her. He seemed content in her arms, snuggled against her, snoozing as he chose, but taking comfort from her body heat. 'I've tried to rent out the other half but no one wants to live this far out of town. So now I'm closing rooms so I won't need to dust.'

'Won't it feel creepy when it's empty?' Bailey asked. 'Like our place does?'

'Ah, but you've forgotten, I have a watchdog now. Ketchup's messed with my plans but now he's here I can make use of him.'

'Were you thinking of moving somewhere smaller?' Nick asked, and she gave him a look that said he didn't get it.

'I told you. I want a yurt. But I'm amenable. Is this all you want? If we're done, then how about tea?'

'You can't be hungry again.'

'How can you doubt it? It's four hours since my sandwich.'

Four hours! Where had the time gone? In drawing yurts. In exploring. In just...talking.

'I'd like a picnic on the beach,' she said and visions of gingham baskets rose again—to be squashed before they hit knee height.

'There's a great pizza place in town,' she said. 'I bribe them to deliver all the way out here.'

'Pizza,' Bailey said with joy, and Ketchup's ears attempted to rise.

'We've hit a nerve.' She grinned. 'Picnic pizza it is. If that's okay with you, Mr Holt?'

'Nick,' he said and it was almost savage.

* * *

She made him take three trips to her favourite spot on the sand dunes, carrying cushions, rugs and food, because she was carrying Ketchup.

They ate pizza until it was coming out of their ears. Ketchup ate pizza, too.

'I have a feeling Ketchup's met pizza in a former life,' Misty said, watching in satisfaction as he nibbled round the edges of a Capriccioso.

'He looks like he might be a nice dog,' Nick said—cautiously. He was feeling cautious.

He was feeling strange.

Ketchup and Bailey were lying full length on the rug. They were playing a gentle boy-dog game that had them touching noses, touching finger to paw, touching paw to finger, then nose to nose again. They were totally absorbed in each other. Bailey was giggling and Ketchup seemed at peace.

The evening was warm and still. The sun was sinking low behind the sand hills and the outgoing tide sent a soft hush-hush of surf over the wet sand. Sandpipers were sweeping up the beach as the water washed in, then scuttling out after the waves to see what had been washed bare.

Misty's house looked out over paradise.

How could a man want adventure when he had this?

And this woman… She was watching Bailey with contentment. She seemed secure in herself, a woman at peace.

She was so different from Isabelle. A woman like this would never need adrenalin rush, danger.

A woman like this…

'Why don't you have a dog already?' he asked and Misty stopped squashing pizza boxes, glanced at Ketchup and looked rueful.

'We had a surfeit of dogs.'

'Who's we?'

'My grandparents and me.'

He thought about that. It seemed safer than the other direction his thoughts were taking. Actually, he wasn't sure where his thoughts were taking him, only that it seemed wise to deflect them. 'Not your parents?'

'My mother didn't live here.'

'Never?'

'Not since she was eighteen. She left to see the world, then turned up only for brief visits, bringing things home. Weird people, artwork, dream-catchers. One day she brought me home.

She didn't stay any longer than the time she brought the dream-catchers, but she left me for good. Gran and Grandpa kept the dream-catchers and they kept me.'

'That sounds dreadful.'

'Does it?' She smiled and ran her fingers the length of Ketchup's spine, causing the little dog to roll his eyes in pleasure. 'It never seemed dreadful. Sad, yes, but not dreadful. We saw her world through postcards, and that gave me a presence to cling to. An identity. And, as for needing her...I wasn't deserted. Gran and Grandpa did everything they could for their daughter, and they did everything they could for me.'

'But you stayed, while your mother left.'

'I loved my grandparents, and they loved me,' she said, sounding suddenly uncompromising. 'That's something I don't think my mother's capable of. It took me a while to figure it out but I know it now.' Her smile faded. 'It's her loss. Loving's fine. Like I fell in love with Ketchup yesterday. I'm a soft touch.'

'You've never fallen in love before?'

'With other dogs?' That wasn't what he'd meant but maybe she'd purposely misunderstood. 'Of course I have. Five years ago we had four. The last one died six months ago. He's buried under Gran's Peace rose in the back garden. And now Gran herself...'

But something there gave her pause. She gave herself a shake, regrouped, obviously changed direction. 'No. Gran's okay. She's had a couple of strokes. She's in a nursing home but she's only seventy-three. I thought... When she had the second stroke and our last dog died I thought...'

Pause. Another shake.

'Well, it doesn't matter what I thought,' she said, almost to herself. 'It's right to get another dog. When you fall in love, what choice do you have?'

'There's always a choice.'

'Like you could walk away from Bailey?' Bailey looked up at that, and she grinned. 'See? I defy you not to love that look.'

'My son's look?'

'Your son.'

'How can you compare a dog...?'

'Love's love,' she said simply. 'You take it where you find it.'

Where he found it? He'd thought he had it with Isabelle. He'd been out of his mind.

Bailey stretched out and yawned. The sun was sinking low in the evening sky.

Misty sat and watched the sandpipers, and he thought she was such a peaceful woman. She was also beautiful. And the more he looked… She was quite astonishingly beautiful.

He wanted, quite badly, to kiss her.

And that was a really bad idea. This was his son's schoolteacher. His son was two feet away.

But not to touch her seemed impossible.

Her hand was on the rug, only inches from his. How could he not? He reached out and ran his fingers gently over the back of her hand and she didn't flinch.

Her skin wasn't silk-smooth like Isabelle's had been. There were tiny scars. Life lines.

The world was still. Maybe…

'No,' she told him and tugged her hand away.

'No?' The contact had been a feather touch, no more. But she'd said no, and even now he knew her well enough to realise that she meant it. And for him? No was sensible. What was he thinking of?

'Parent-teacher relationships are disasters,' she said.

'Always?' The word was out before he could stop it.

'Always.'

'You've tried a few?'

'That's my business.'

He smiled but it was an effort, and that was a puzzle on its own. What was happening here? He had to get this back on a lighter note.

'I've told you about Isabelle,' he said, in a dare you tone.

'You want me to tell you about Roger Proudy kissing me behind the shelter sheds when I was eight?'

'Did he?'

'Yes, and it was sloppy.' She was also striving to make this light, he thought. That was good. She had a handle on things, which was more than he did.

'When Grandma kisses me it's sloppy,' Bailey said dreamily from where he was snoozing against Ketchup, and the conversation suddenly lost its intensity. They were back on a plane where he could keep his balance.

'Do you have one grandma or two?' Misty asked Bailey.

'Two, but Grandma Holt cries, and she gets lip-
stick all over me.'

'That sounds yuck,' Misty said. 'Do you see
your grandmas often?'

'Gran Rose and Papa Bill live on a boat like
we used to,' Bailey said. 'They came to see me
in hospital lots of times. They gave me computer
games and stuff. But Grandma and Grandpa Holt
only came once. Grandma said computer games
are the work of the devil, and Grandpa yelled
at Dad when he said we weren't going back to
Pen…Pennsylvania. Then Grandma Holt cried,
and kissed me too hard, and it was really, really
sloppy.'

'Double yuck.' Misty smiled, then turned to
Nick, her eyes lighting with laughter. 'Would
Grandma Holt be the no risk grandma? Someone
should tell her you can share germs with sloppy
kisses.'

And suddenly Nick found himself grinning.

The decision to bring Bailey to Australia had
been made under all sorts of constraints. If he'd
returned to the States, his parents would have
given him a hard time. They'd give Bailey a hard
time. But if he'd stayed in England…

Isabelle's parents were based in England. They

loved Bailey desperately, but loving had its own challenges. They'd smother Bailey, he thought, and maybe Bailey would react as Isabelle had reacted.

Since Isabelle's death, he'd been in a haze of grief and self-blame. Banksia Bay offered a new start. Here, they were away from Isabelle's parents, with their indulgence. They were away from his own parents saying the things they'd always said, only this time with the rider: 'I told you so.'

Moving to Banksia Bay meant Bailey was spared sloppy kisses.

He looked at Misty and he thought…kisses equal germs?

His grin faded.

'We need to go home,' he said, and he knew he sounded harsh but he couldn't help himself. What he was feeling was suddenly pushing him right out of his comfort zone. This was his kid's schoolteacher. He'd touched her. He shouldn't have touched her.

He shouldn't want to touch her.

But she was right beside him, and she was warm, open and loving in a way he could only sense. She was smiling a question at him now, wondering at the sudden change in his tone.

She wouldn't react with anger, he thought, flashing back to Isabelle's moments of fury, of unreasonable temper. Here was a woman who saw everything on an equable plane. Who moved through life with serenity and peace.

And beauty. She really was beautiful, he thought. Those eyes…those curls…

No. He had to leave.

'We need to get moving,' he told his son, rising too fast. 'Let's get this gear up to the house and go.'

'I don't want to go home.' Bailey's voice was slurred by sleep. He was nestled against Ketchup, peaceful now as he hadn't been peaceful for a year. Or more. Maybe never? 'Why can't we stay here?'

'We can't sleep on the beach.'

'I mean in Miss Lawrence's house.' It was as if Bailey was dreaming, drifting into fantasy. 'I could sleep in one of her big, big beds. Me and Ketchup. I could see Ketchup every morning.'

What the…? The idea took his breath away. 'Miss Lawrence doesn't want us here.'

'Ketchup wants us here.'

'No,' Misty said, sounding strange. She also rose, and she looked just as taken aback as he was. 'That's not a good idea, Bailey. You have a house.'

But suddenly Bailey was fully awake, sitting up, considering his suggestion with care. 'Our house is horrid. And we could help look after Ketchup.'

'I can look after Ketchup on my own.'

'He likes me.'

'I know he does,' she said. She stooped and hugged Bailey, then lifted Ketchup into her arms. 'But Ketchup's my dog. Your dad's paid his bills and that's all the help I'll ask. I look after Gran and I look after Ketchup. I can't look after anyone else. I'm sorry, but you and your dad are on your own.'

CHAPTER FIVE

SHE needed to visit Gran. She needed to find her balance.

Once Nick and Bailey were out of sight she settled Ketchup back into her car. He'd be best off sleeping in his basket at home, but every time she walked away he started shaking.

She could worry about Ketchup. She couldn't worry about Bailey and his father.

She couldn't think about Bailey's father.

Was it only yesterday she'd been celebrating Adonis arriving in her classroom? One touch and her equilibrium was shattered.

Think about the dog. Much, much safer.

'You've sucked me in,' she murmured. 'Where did you come from, and how exposed have you made me? Oh, Ketchup.'

But he hadn't made her exposed—he'd simply shown her what life was. Yurts were fantasy. Ketchup was real.

Bailey was real.

She was a total sucker.

'I'm sorry, but you and your dad are on your own.' She'd watched Bailey's face as she'd said it and she'd seen him become...stoical.

She'd been stoical at six. For all her bravado about not needing her mother...surviving on post-cards had hardly been survival at all.

She'd ached to go with her. Other kids had mothers. She'd got postcards in the mail.

Bailey got nothing.

He had his dad. It was more than she'd ever had.

No, she told herself sharply. She'd had grand-parents who loved her. But grandparents never, ever made up for what a mother was supposed to be. She had a clear idea of what was right, even at six.

'So you're thinking you can possibly turn your-self into a substitute mother for Bailey? Take them in and coddle them?

'Of course I can't.' She was talking to herself, out loud, the habit of a woman who lived alone.

'Why not? The place they're in is awful. You've been looking for tenants for months. Bailey would love living with Ketchup. Why reject them out of hand?

'Because Nicholas scares me.'

Think about it.

She did think.

She couldn't stop thinking.

She was out of her mind.

'Why can't we live with Miss Lawrence?'

There were a million reasons. He couldn't tell his son any of them.

Except one.

'You heard her. She said no. I think Miss Lawrence likes living alone.'

'She doesn't. She said she tried to rent part of her house. And we wouldn't have to move furniture.'

Why was he blessed with a smart kid with big ears?

'Maybe she wants a single person. Maybe another lady.'

'We're better than a lady.' Bailey wriggled down into his seat and thought about it. 'It'd be good. I really like Ketchup.'

Nick thought Ketchup was okay, too. Ketchup and Bailey touching noses. Bailey truly happy for the first time since his mother died. Ketchup had made him smile.

'Maybe we could get our own dog,' he said and then he heard what he'd said and couldn't believe it.

Here was a perfect example of mouth operating before head. Was he out of his mind? Where were his resolutions?

But he'd said it, and it was too late to haul it back. Bailey's face lit like a Christmas tree. 'We can get a dog?' he breathed.

'Maybe we can,' he said, feeling winded. 'Seeing as we can't live with Miss Lawrence.'

But Bailey had moved past Miss Lawrence. He was only seeing four legs and a tail. 'I can have a dog of my own?'

Miss Lawrence had a lot to answer for, he decided. His plans had *not* included a dog. 'A young dog,' he said. That, at least, was sensible. A young healthy dog wouldn't cause grief. A young dog *probably* wouldn't cause grief.

He'd have to reinforce fences, he thought. He'd have to keep the dog safe, too.

'He'll be able to play with Ketchup,' Bailey said, not hearing his reservations. He was almost rigid with excitement. 'Do you think we can find a dog who'll touch noses? Me and Ketchup touch noses. Like you and Miss Lawrence touch hands.'

'That's got nothing to do…'

But Bailey wasn't listening. The touching hands thing was simply a passing fact. 'Dogs are great,' he said, breathless and wondering. This was turning into a very good day in the World According to Bailey, and he was starting to plan. 'We'll be able to take our dog to visit Ketchup. We'll all have picnics on the beach. We'll all still be able to touch.'

What was a man to say to that?

'Can we build a kennel?'

'I…yes.'

'I can't wait to tell Miss Lawrence,' Bailey said.

'We may not see Miss Lawrence until Monday.'

'We need to get our furniture,' Bailey said happily. 'We'll see her tomorrow. Can we get a dog tomorrow?'

'Do you think having Nicholas Holt and his son as tenants is a bad idea?'

It *was* a bad idea. There were complications on every side. She shouldn't even think it but Bailey's expression wouldn't go away. Bailey's need.

What was it in him that had touched such a chord within?

Other kids lost mothers.

It was the way he'd touched noses with Ketchup, she thought. She'd watched him find huge pleasure in that simple contact, and she remembered how important dogs had been to her as a child. Bailey couldn't go his whole life without a mother—and without a dog.

If they became her tenants he'd share Ketchup. Ketchup would be on Bailey's bed in no time. Kid and dog. Perfect fit.

Their house was truly appalling. Bailey's suggestion was even sensible.

If only she could ignore Nicholas.

She was a grown woman. Could a grown woman get her hormones under control enough to consider a sensible plan?

Surely she could.

Misty set the whole thing in front of Gran, and Gran considered it. Misty knew she did. Gran did a lot of considering these days.

Gran's eyes were closed tonight but, when Misty settled Ketchup on her bedclothes, against Gran's hand, she saw Gran's fingers move against his furry coat. Just a little, convulsively, as if she was remembering something she'd forgotten.

Gran loved dogs.

Love was a dangerous concept, Misty thought. She'd fallen for Ketchup, she was falling for Bailey, and where were her plans now? In a muddle, that was where.

'I shouldn't have agreed to keep Ketchup.'

Gran's fingers moved again.

'You're a soft touch, too. We both are.' She lifted Gran's spare hand to her cheek. 'Oh, Gran, this is dumb. I have fallen for Ketchup, and I would like someone living in the other side of my house. Bailey needs a good place to live and it's sensible. It's just…Nick touched me. I'm scared I'll get involved and I want to be free. But free's not an option. I'm being dumb.'

She had to let her plans go.

She already had, she thought, or she almost had, the moment she'd fallen for Ketchup. And maybe letting her plans go was her only option.

Six months ago, the doctors had told her Gran had weeks to live. But Gran was still here, and there was no thought of her dying. And in the end… How could Misty possibly dream of a future with Gran not here?

Ketchup was deeply asleep now. He'd had a huge day for an injured dog. She should have him at home, right now.

'It's okay to live alone,' she told her grand-mother. 'I don't need anyone to help me care for Ketchup, and I don't need complications.'

Gran's hand slid sideways. The tiny moment of awareness was gone.

Misty's thoughts telescoped, out of frame. To a future without Gran?

She'd thought of what she'd do when Gran was gone, but now…Gran was here but not here, and she could well be like this for years.

The future looked terrifying. Living in that great house alone. Never leaving this town.

What to do?

Since Gran's first stroke she'd been trying to plan, trying to figure her future. But in truth she'd been planning since before she could remember. Making lists.

Maybe she should stop planning and just…be.

She wouldn't mind Nicholas and his little son living next door. It wasn't exactly a bleak thought.

She wouldn't need to rush home to feed Ketchup on nights when she had to stay back at school.

That was a sensible thought.

And then… Another sensible thought. The re-surgence of the dream.

'You know, if anything happened to Gran,' she told Ketchup as she settled him back into her car. 'Just saying… If it did, and if Nicholas and Bailey were living in my house… They could look after you while I tried out a yurt. Just for a while.'

Yes. Her dream re-emerged, dusted itself off, settled back into the corner of her mind, where it had been a comfort for years.

'You're making me realign my existence,' she told Ketchup. 'Two days ago, I was alone. What are you doing with my life?'

Ketchup looked at her and shifted his tail, just a little, but enough to make her smile. She did want this dog.

'Maybe you're my nemesis,' she told him. 'I thought Gran's death would be the thing that changed my life. Maybe it's you.'

She bent over to hug him and got a lick for her pains.

'Enough.' She chuckled. 'I'm not used to kisses.'

A kiss. A touch? She was thinking again of Nick's hand on hers. The strength of his fingers. The warmth of skin against skin.

Ketchup wasn't her only nemesis. There was something about Nicholas that was messing with her plans in a far bigger way. In a way that was much more threatening.

She had to be sensible, she told herself. She had a dog and a grandmother and a house that was too big for her. And if there was something about Nicholas that scared her…

Yep, she just had to be sensible.

He'd agreed to get a dog.

Bailey had gone to sleep planning dog kennels. Tomorrow they'd build a kennel and they'd start to make this place habitable. They were settled. Here.

He'd leased this place for three months. He'd find somewhere else after that, maybe near the school. It'd be okay.

He and Bailey and dog—a young healthy dog— could live happily ever after.

So what was there in that to make him stare up at the ceiling and think…and think…?

And think of Misty.

She tossed the concept around all night and in the morning there was only one answer.

So ask him. Now, before she chickened out.

She didn't have Nick's cellphone number. She

could go into school and fetch his parent file, only she'd have to drive past his house to get it. Which was stupid. Cowardly, even.

Ketchup was deeply asleep. She'd had him in a basket beside her bed all night. At dawn he'd stirred. She'd taken him outside and he'd smelled the sea and sniffed the grass. He looked a hundred per cent on yesterday. She'd cuddled him and cooked them both breakfast. He'd eaten two bacon rashers and half a cup of dog food and returned to his basket.

He was now fast asleep on Gran's old woollen cardigan and he didn't look as if he'd stir any time soon.

Unlike Misty, who was stirring so much she felt as if she was going nuts.

It was eight o'clock. The world must surely be awake.

So ask him *now*.

He heard the knock as he stood under the shower. Which was cold. The hot water service gave exactly thirty seconds of tepid water. 'Bailey…'

'I heard,' Bailey yelled, sounding excited, which was pretty much how he'd sounded since Nick had said the D word last night.

'Don't answer it.' He groped for his towel, swearing under his breath. It could be anyone out there. *Do not take risks.*

'Bailey, don't…' he yelled again but it was too late. There was a whoop of pleasure from the hall.

'It's Miss Lawrence. Dad, it's Miss Lawrence. She's come to visit.'

Bailey was still in his pyjamas, clutching his teddy, rumpled from sleep. He was beaming with pleasure to see her. He looked adorable.

He also looked big with news. He was jiggling up and down, stammering with excitement.

'I'm getting a dog,' he told her before she could say a word, and she blinked in astonishment.

'A what?'

'A dog.' He did another jig. 'We've talked about it. I think we should look at the lost dogs' home 'cos Dad says Ketchup was from the dogs' home and he's good. But I want a dog who can run. Dad says I can choose but he can't be old. And he can't be sick. We're going to build a dog kennel, only Dad says he doesn't know if we can buy wood and stuff on Sunday.'

His joy was enough to make the hardest heart

melt, and Misty's wasn't all that hard to start with. A dog of his own…

This little boy had lost his mother in dreadful circumstances. His only friend was his father. But now… To have his own dog…

'That's…' But she never got to answer.

Nick strode from the bathroom, snapping orders. 'Bailey, don't answer the door to strangers…'

He was wearing nothing but boxers.

Misty was a woman with sound feminist principles. She didn't gasp. She didn't even let her knees buckle, which she discovered they were more than willing to do. Women with feminist principles did not gasp at the sight of near naked men. Nor did they allow their knees to buckle, even if they wanted to.

Nick had towelled in a hurry and he wasn't quite dry. His bare tanned chest was still wet. More, it sort of glistened under the hall light. This was a male body which belonged…which belonged somewhere else but in her universe.

'H…hi,' she managed, and was inordinately proud she'd made her voice work.

'It's Miss Lawrence,' Bailey told Nick unnecessarily. He was still jiggling. 'I told her we're getting a dog.'

'Why are you here?' There was a pause, and Nick seemed to collect himself. It was possible he hadn't intended to sound as if she might be a child-snatcher. He took a deep breath, started again. 'Sorry. Obviously I need to get used to country hours. So...' He hesitated and tried a smile. 'You've already milked the cows, churned the butter...'

'Swilled the pigs and chewed the buttercups,' she agreed, managing to smile back. She might be disconcerted, but Nick looked even more disconcerted. Which was kind of...nice. To have such a body disconcerted because of her...

Get serious, she told herself, but it was really hard to be serious in the face of those pecs.

'It's me who should be sorry,' she managed. 'Ketchup woke me at dawn and I've been thinking. Actually, I was even thinking last night.'

'Thinking?'

'That maybe I was wrong to knock Bailey back so fast. 'That maybe it's not a bad idea at all. That maybe it might suit us all if you share my house.'

Silence.

More silence.

Whatever reaction she'd expected, it wasn't this.

Nick was staring at her as if he wasn't quite sure who—or what—she was.

As well he might. He'd only met her yesterday. What sort of offer was this?

But they didn't need to be friends to be a landlady and tenant, she reminded herself. They hardly needed to know each other. This was business.

Still there was silence. She wasn't quite sure how to break it, and finally Bailey did it for her. 'We can live with you?' he breathed, and his question hauled her straight down to earth.

Uh oh. Stupid, stupid, stupid. This was not strictly business. Here was the first complication. A basic principle of teaching: don't make children excited before plans are definite. She and Nick should have had this conversation out of Bailey's hearing.

What had she been thinking, just to blurt it out?

She knew what she'd been thinking about. This was all about Nicholas Holt's wet, glistening body. It had knocked the sense right out of her. Understandably, she decided. There was something about Nicholas Holt that was enough to throw any right-minded woman off balance.

'If your father thinks it's a good idea,' she

managed, struggling to make it good. She allowed herself to glance again at that glistening body and she thought maybe she'd made a king-sized fool of herself.

He was still looking at her as if she'd grown two heads. That was what she felt like, she decided. As if there was the one-headed Miss Lawrence, the woman who made sense. And the two-headed one who was making all sorts of mistakes.

No matter. She'd made her offer.

If he wanted to live with a two-headed twit then she'd left herself open for it to happen.

She was asking him to live with her?

No. She was asking if he'd like to rent the spare side of her gorgeous house.

Nick was cold. This house was cold.

He'd tried to make toast and the fuse had blown. Half the house was now without electricity. He'd checked the fuse box and what he saw there made him wince. This house wasn't just bad, it was teetering on unsafe.

There were possums—or rats—in the roof. He'd lain awake all night trying to decide which.

A breeze was coming up through the floor-boards.

This was not a suitable house for Bailey. He'd made that decision at about four o'clock this morning in between muttering invective at possums. He needed to go find the letting agent, throw back his keys, threaten to sue him for false advertising, find somewhere else...

Before tonight?

But here was Misty, warm and smiling and friendly, saying come and live in her house, with her squishy old furniture, with a veranda that looked over the sea, with Misty herself...

Um...take Misty out of the equation fast, he told himself. This was a business proposition. A good one?

Maybe it was. It'd get him out of immediate trouble. To have his son warm and comfortable and safe...

He wouldn't need to get a dog.

He looked down at Bailey. Bailey looked up at him with eyes that were pure pleading.

A comfortable house by the sea. No dog. Misty.

This was a very sensible plan.

'We accept.'

He accepted? Just like that? The two words

seemed to make Misty's insides jolt. What had she just done?

But Nick was sounding cautious, as well he might. *She* was feeling cautious. What sort of crazy impulse had led her here?

For, as soon as he accepted, complications crowded in. Or maybe as soon as she'd seen his wet body complications had crowded in, but she'd been so overwhelmed she'd made the offer before she thought.

And now…

Now he'd accepted. Warily. So where to take it from here?

This was still sensible, she told herself. Stick to business. She needed to avoid looking at his body and remember what she'd planned to say.

'You might need to think about it,' she managed. 'You…you'll need to agree to my rent. And we'd need to set up rules. We'd live on opposite sides of the house. You'd look after yourselves. No shared cooking or housework. Separate households. I'm not turning into your housekeeper.'

'I wouldn't expect you to.' He raked his fingers through his damp hair, looking flummoxed. 'You're serious?'

'I think I am.' Was she serious? She was

probably seriously nuts—but how did a girl back out now?

She couldn't.

A sudden gust of wind hit the outside of the house and blew straight through the floorboards. This house was colder inside than out, she thought. Bailey shouldn't be here and Nick knew it.

'Would there be gossip?' he asked.

So he knew how small towns worked. He was right. In most small towns, gossip would be an issue.

But there was never gossip about *her*, Misty thought, feeling suddenly bitter. She was Banksia Bay's good girl. It'd take more than one man and his son to mess with the stereotype the locals had created for her.

'It'll be fine,' she told him. 'The town knows I'm respectable and they know I've been looking for a tenant for months. And people already know about Bailey. Believe it or not, I've had four phone calls already saying how can you—*you*, Nicholas Holt—take care of a recuperating child in this house, and why don't I take pity on you and ask you to move into my place?'

And every one of those calls had been engineered by Fred. The old vet was a Machiavellian busybody.

She loved him to bits.

'So all I need to do is tell the people who've suggested it how brilliant they are,' she added.

And keep this businesslike, she added to herself, because, respectable or not, any sniff of anything else would get around so fast...

But, in truth, Banksia Bay might decide *anything else* was a good thing, she thought, letting herself wallow in bitterness a bit longer. The locals knew of her dreams, but they flatly rejected the idea she could ever leave. They'd approve of anything that kept her here.

Despite that, she was still fighting to get herself free. And this could help. Having people share her house. Share Ketchup.

Businesslike was the way to go, she told herself again. Adonis or not, involvement messed with her dreams.

As did the sight of Nicholas Holt's bare chest.

But in her silence Nick had been thinking. 'It could work well,' he said slowly. 'We can share Ketchup.'

Here was an echo of her thoughts. 'Share?'

'I told Bailey if we didn't move into your house we'd get a dog.'

'Dad...' Bailey said, unsure.

'We don't need our own dog if we have Ketchup,' Nick said.

And all the colour went from Bailey's face, just like that. All the joy. He'd opened the door for Misty looking puffed up like a peacock, a six-year-old with all the pleasure in the world before him.

Right now, he looked as if he'd been slapped.

'But you said,' Bailey whispered. Nick had seen Bailey's colour fade. In two strides he was beside him, lifting him up into his arms. Holding him close. 'Don't you want to stay with Miss Lawrence and Ketchup?' he asked.

'Yes, but I want a dog of my very own,' Bailey whispered.

'We don't need...' Nick started but Misty shook her head. She'd looked at Bailey and thought yes, he does. He does need a dog of his own.

Sharing wouldn't cut it.

Misty had had a solitary childhood, living out of town with her elderly, invalid grandparents. Her dogs had meant everything to her.

Last night she'd seen an echo of that. Noses on the beach. Ketchup.

Bailey was a great kid. She knew him well enough to realise he'd take great care of a dog.

So say it.

'What if I give you Ketchup?' she said, and both guys looked at her as if she'd just declared she was selling her grandmother.

'But Ketchup's yours,' Bailey whispered, appalled. 'He knows he is. He told me.'

'I've only just got him,' Misty said gently. 'He doesn't really know me. You and Ketchup had a wonderful game on the beach last night.'

'I want my dog and Ketchup to be friends.'

And Nick obviously had qualms as well, but they were different qualms. 'The vet says Ketchup's close to ten years old,' he said.

Now it was Misty's turn to look at Nick as if he was selling *his* grandmother.

'So?'

'So he'll…'

'He'll what?' she said dangerously.

'If we must get a dog, we'll get a young one. Ketchup will cause you grief.'

'Everyone causes you grief,' she said. 'That's

what loving's about. Like you. You love Bailey so you promised him a dog.'

'I didn't actually promise.'

'You did,' Bailey said and buried his face in his father's shoulder.

'I believe I said if we didn't live with Miss Lawrence.'

His explanation didn't help at all. Bailey's sob was truly heart-rending—and Nicholas looked at her as if she'd personally caused this.

Enough. This was crazy. She was starting to feel as if she was causing nothing but heartache.

The sight of Nick hugging Bailey was doing weird things to her. Nick with his gorgeous body. Nick with the way he loved his son.

And Bailey? Somehow this small boy had managed to twist his way right around her heart.

Bailey's pyjama sleeve was hitched up as he clung round his father's neck. She could see the savage mark of the bullet, and the scars from the surgery after.

She was messing with Bailey by being here, she decided. Nick had had this sorted, and now she'd come in with an offer that was messing with Bailey's dreams.

Nick would find somewhere else to live. She

didn't actually need these two guys in her house. Not if it messed with dreams.

'I believe I need to rescind,' she said before she could think it through any further.

'Sorry?' Nick sounded stunned.

'My offer is withdrawn.' She took a deep breath and met his gaze square on. 'Bailey needs a dog.'

'Not if he gets to share yours.'

'He's not sharing mine. I no longer want you as tenants. Not if it means Bailey misses out on a dog of his own.'

Once again, that look as if she had two heads. 'This is ridiculous.'

'It is,' she said, but then she thought that it wasn't. She thought of the white-faced little boy on Friday night, grabbing his teddy as soon as he got home. She thought of him last night on the beach, touching noses with Ketchup.

A dog of his own would be perfect.

But Nick's face…

How had this happened? He was stuck if he did, and stuck if he didn't.

So help him out. Make his decision for him. She'd always fought for her students' needs. For

Bailey, there was never going to be a better time to fight than right now.

'So you're saying…' Nicholas said slowly.

'That I'm no longer offering you my house. Unless,' she said softly, watching Bailey, 'Bailey has his own dog.'

Nick's face turned to thunder.

'Henrietta Farnsworth runs the Animal Welfare,' she said, briskly efficient now she saw her way. Or Nick's way. 'It's only open weekdays, but on Sundays she feeds and cleans at eleven. You could go choose a dog and then accept my very kind offer by midday.'

'This is blackmail.' Nick's growl was truly menacing, but Bailey had turned to look at her and his look strengthened her resolve. She grinned at Bailey and she winked.

'I agree with Bailey. He needs his own dog.'

'Dogs cause you grief. I don't want Bailey to face that kind of hurt.'

'You're saying you won't get a dog because eventually you might lose him? What sort of argument is that? You're living in the country now. Country kids know about birth and death. Natalie's dad's cow lost one of her twins yesterday. Natalie will tell everyone all the gory details on Monday morning. It's sad but it happens. You can't shield Bailey for ever. Choose a young dog and take your chances.'

Silence. She let the silence run.

Nick set Bailey down and Bailey had the sense to remain silent. Nick raked his fingers through his hair again. She'd first noticed him doing it yesterday, when he was drawing his plans for her yurt. His long strong fingers, running through thick wavy hair, had made her feel… Was making her feel…

Uh oh. Let's not go there.

But she was there. Maybe this man was going to live just through the wall from her.

She shivered, but not with cold.

But he was still coming at her with arguments. 'I didn't mean to promise Bailey a dog,' he started.

She was ready for him this time, growing firmer. 'Yes, you did or you wouldn't have said it.'

'It was a rash moment.'

'You'll love a dog. You saw Ketchup and Bailey together. You'll both love a dog.'

'But Ketchup's recuperating.' He was starting to sound helpless. Helpless and sexy. It seemed an incredibly appealing, incredibly masculine combination.

Stop it. She was a respectable schoolteacher, she told herself. She was a potential landlady. Listen to what he's saying.

'Ketchup doesn't need company.' His arguments were getting weaker.

'Ketchup doesn't need a rough companion,' she agreed. 'Or not at first. But we can keep them separate. Like you and I will be separate. I want tenants, not friends.'

'Really?'

She drew her breath in on that one. *Really?*

'We can meet on the veranda occasionally,' she conceded.

'And Bailey can play with Ketchup,' he said, fast. 'See, he doesn't need a dog of his own.'

'I do,' Bailey said.

'He does,' she said. 'But this is no longer my call. Talk to your son about it. I'm happy to welcome you, your son and your dog into my house, or I'm happy to continue living alone. I need to check on Ketchup. Let me know.'

Enough. She'd thrown her hat into the ring.

Now it was up to him.

'Up to you,' she said and she turned and walked back down the veranda steps and drove away.

What had she done?

Nicholas Holt had just backed himself into a very small corner.

Maybe he'd be angry. Maybe he'd decide that yes, he'd buy a dog, but they wouldn't move into her place. If he thought she was a blackmailer, they just might.

Maybe he'd tell Bailey that yes, he'd buy him a dog, but not till, say, Christmas. Or when he reached twenty-one.

Ketchup was awake and watching for her. He hopped stiffly out of his basket, balancing on three legs as he nudged her ankles. He had a world of worry in his eyes.

'That makes two of us worried. But I don't know why I am,' she told him. 'I don't want them to move here. It'd cause complications.'

But she was lying. She did want them to move here. She wanted complications.

'Only because I can't have my yurt for a while longer,' she muttered. 'I need to let it go.'

She had let it go. And maybe she'd just let prospective tenants go.

'I've pushed him too far,' she told Ketchup.

Maybe he wasn't as wealthy as the Internet suggested. She knew the guy who owned the house he was in. He'd have demanded rent in advance.

Nick was already paying an expensive veterinary bill. He hadn't asked her how much she intended charging. Maybe…Maybe…

Maybe she was a complete fool. And the way he made her feel… What was she doing, hoping the phone would ring?

The phone rang.

She let it ring five times. It wouldn't do to be eager.

On the sixth ring she lifted it. 'Yes?' She was gearing herself for a blunt refusal. Anger. Maybe he had the right to be angry.

'You need to help me,' Nick said, sounding goaded.

'How can I do that?'

'You need to help my son choose a dog,' he said. 'What time did you say this woman will be at the Shelter? And then you need to give me a key to your front door. I believe you have two new tenants. Three, if you count our new dog.'

CHAPTER SIX

NICK drove towards the Animal Shelter and beside him Bailey's face glowed. He held his teddy, but he was looking forward, all eagerness, to what lay ahead.

'A dog of my own,' he whispered as if he couldn't believe what was happening. 'And living with Miss Lawrence...'

'*Next door* to Miss Lawrence.'

'I know,' he said. 'I'm getting a dog.'

Dogs had germs. Nick could still hear the echo of his mother's horrified response when he'd asked for a dog thirty years ago.

Germs. Heartbreak. Loss. This was a risk—but Misty was right. He couldn't protect his son from everything. He needed to loosen up.

And his son would be safe with Misty. The sensation that caused was wonderful. It was like going into freefall, but knowing the landing was assured. And maybe the landing was more wonderful than the fall itself.

For, dog or not, once he'd agreed to her conditions, he felt as if he was landing. He was finding a home for his son—with Misty.

He was finding a home *beside* Misty, he reminded himself, but that wasn't how his body was thinking.

She'd teased him this morning. She'd backed him into a corner and she'd enjoyed doing it.

He'd been angry, frustrated, baffled—but he'd loved her doing it.

He turned the corner and she was already parked outside the Shelter. She was standing in the dappled sunlight under a vast gum tree, in her faded jeans, a sleeveless gingham shirt and old trainers. Her hair was caught back with a red ribbon and the sunlight was making her chestnut curls shine.

'Isn't she pretty?' Bailey whispered and he could only agree.

Beautiful.

'She has Ketchup,' his son added, and Bailey was right. She had her dog in her arms. Why did she have him here?

'We need Ketchup's approval,' she explained. 'If these dogs are to live next door, we can't have them growling at each other.'

'I want a running dog,' Bailey said.

'Fast is good,' Misty agreed. She wasn't looking at Nick. Her attention was totally on Bailey and he was caught by the fact that he was sidelined.

From the time he'd won his first design prize, aged all of nineteen, Nick had moved among some of the wealthiest women in the world. His boat owners had money to burn and the boats he designed meant he had money to match them.

Women reacted to him. Even when he'd been married, women had taken notice of him. But now it was clear he came a poor second to his son and he thought the better of her for it.

More than that, the sensation had him feeling… Feeling…

Now's hardly the time to think about how you're feeling, he told himself. Not when you're about to move next door to her. You're here to choose a dog for your son.

'Let's get this over with,' he muttered, and Misty looked at him in astonishment.

'Don't sound so severe. This isn't a trip to the dentist.'

'It might as well be.'

She'd started walking towards the Shelter but his words stopped her. She turned and met his gaze full on. Carefully, she set Ketchup down on the grass and she disengaged her hand from Bailey's.

'If you really don't want a dog, then stop right now,' she said, her voice suddenly steely. 'The dogs in the Shelter have had a tough time—they've been abandoned already. They don't want a half-hearted owner. Bailey, if your daddy doesn't really want a dog, then of course I won't insist. You can still share my house, and you and I can share Ketchup.'

She was angry?

She was definitely angry.

'I got it wrong,' she told him, still in that cold voice. 'I thought it was just your stupid qualms about germs and risks. But if it's more…say it now, Nicholas, and we'll all go home. Bailey, if your father doesn't really want a dog, honestly, could you be happy with Ketchup?'

Bailey stared up at her, surprised. He looked down at Ketchup, who looked back at him. Kid and dog.

'Dad says we can have a dog,' he whispered.

'He needs to prove it. Why don't we leave it for a bit so he can make up his mind? Owning your own dog is a big thing. I'm not sure your dad's ready for it.'

He was a bright kid, was Bailey, and he knew the odds. He looked up at Nick and he tilted his chin. And then, surprisingly, he tucked his hand into Misty's.

'It's okay,' he told his father. He swallowed manfully. 'Miss Lawrence and I can share looking after Ketchup.' He sounded as if he was placating someone the same age as he was—or younger. 'If you really, really, really don't want a dog just for us, then it's okay, Dad.' He gulped and clutched his teddy.

It only needed this. Nick closed his eyes. When he opened them, they were still looking at him. Misty and Bailey. And Ketchup. Even Teddy.

If you really, really, really don't want a dog just for us...

Misty's gaze had lost its cool. Now she looked totally non-judgmental. She'd backed right off. She'd given him a way out.

Behind them, a woman was emerging from the Shelter. Glancing across at them. Starting to lock up.

Was this Henrietta, finishing early? She was letting him off the hook as well.

He felt about six inches high.

What had he got himself into?

He glanced once more, at his son and his son's teacher, and suddenly he knew exactly what he was getting into.

'You want to go home?' Misty asked and he shook his head.

'I'm an idiot,' he told her. And then... 'Are you Henrietta?' he called before any more of his stupid scruples could get in the way of what was looking more and more...he didn't know what, but he surely intended to find out.

'Yes,' the woman called back, cautious.

'Can you wait a moment before you lock up?' he asked her. 'If it's okay with you... My son and I are here to see if we can choose a dog. We both want a dog and we're hoping we can find one, right now. A dog that's fast. A dog that's young and a dog who can belong just to Bailey.'

And in the end it was easy.

Misty and Nick left things to Henrietta and Bailey. 'Henrietta knows her dogs,' Misty told Nick. 'She won't introduce him to one that's unsuitable.'

Bailey walked along the pens, looking worried.

He looked at each dog in turn. They barked, they whined or they ignored him, and Bailey looked increasingly unsure.

But then he came to a pen near the end, and he stopped.

'This one's a whippet,' Henrietta said. 'She's fast. She's hardly more than a pup and she's a sweetheart.'

'She's hurt her face,' Bailey whispered.

'Most dogs in here have scars,' Henrietta told him and she was talking to him as if he was an equal and not six years old.

Bailey looked back along the lines of pens— then, as if he'd made some sort of decision, he sat beside the pen with the whippet. The whippet was lying prone on the concrete floor, her nose against the bars, misery personified.

Bailey put his nose against the dog's nose. Testing?

Nick started forward, worried, but Misty put her hand on his arm.

'Trust Henrietta. If she thinks a dog's safe with kids, she'll be right. And did you know kids from farms have twenty per cent fewer allergies than city kids? What's a nose rub between friends?'

Bailey looked back to them, his little face

serious. 'She's skinny,' he said cautiously. 'Can I pat her?'

'Sure you can,' Henrietta said, and Nick and Misty walked forward to see. They reached the cage—and something amazing happened. Ketchup stared down at the whippet from the safety of Misty's arms. He whined—and then suddenly he was a different dog. He was squirming, barking, desperate to get down.

The whippet was stick-thin, fawn with a soft white face, and she was carrying the scars of mistreatment or neglect. She'd been flattened on the floor of the pen, shivering, but as Misty knelt with Ketchup in her arms she lunged forward and hit the bars—and she went wild.

Both dogs did.

They were practically delirious in their excitement. Two dogs with cold bars between them… That these dogs had a shared history was obvious.

'Hey, I'd forgotten. You've brought her friend back.' Henrietta grinned and stooped to scratch Ketchup behind his ears, only Ketchup wasn't noticing. He was too intent on the whippet.

'These two were found together,' Henrietta told them. 'I reckon they were dumped together. We put 'em in pens side by side but they seemed in-separable so they ended up together. Your little guy...' She motioned to Ketchup. 'He's cute and normally we'd have had no problem rehousing him, but no one's wanted the skinny one. And somehow no one wanted to separate them.'

'He's ugly,' Nicholas said, looking at the whip-pet, appalled, and the Shelter worker looked at him as if she wasn't sure where to place him.

'I like whippets,' she said neutrally. 'They're great dogs, intelligent and gentle and fun. Whippets always look skinny, but you're right, this one's ribs practically cross over. She's a she, by the way. She'll feed up, given time, but, of course, they ran out of time. They were both in the van when it crashed on Thursday. Dotty Ludeman found this one in her yard last night and brought her in. So here they are, together again.'

She smiled then, the tentative smile of a true animal-lover who thought she scented a happy ending. 'So Misty's saved one—and your little boy wants the other?'

'I'm not sure.' Nick had visions of some-thing cute. Surely Bailey had visions of some-thing cute.

'Whippets can run,' Bailey breathed.

'How do you know?'

'There was a book about dogs at the hospital,' Bailey told him. '*Whippy the Whippet*. Faster'n a speeding bullet.'

'I know that book,' Misty said. 'Ooh, I bet she could run on our beach.'

Our beach. That sounded okay. Nick crouched to get a better view of the...whippet? He knew zip about dogs.

'She's really skinny,' Bailey said.

'Are you sure she's safe with kids?' Misty asked, and Henrietta chuckled and nodded and opened the cage. The skinny dog wriggled out and wormed ecstatically around Ketchup. Misty and Bailey were sitting on the concrete floor now and the whippet wound round them and back, round them and back. Ketchup whimpered but it was a whimper of delight.

'Uh oh,' Misty said.

'Uh oh?' Nick queried.

'I need to tell you.' She smiled and sighed, letting the whippet nose her way into her arms along with Ketchup. 'What are lists, anyway? If you don't want this little girl, then I do.'

'Do you want her to live on your side of the

wall?' Bailey demanded, watching the skinny dog with fascination.

'If you and your dad don't want her,' she said. 'But if you do…these two are obviously meant to be together.'

'So could we cut a hole straight away?'

'I guess we could,' she said, glancing at Nick. Who was glancing at her. Only he was more than glancing.

She'd take on the world, he thought. She'd taken on Ketchup. She'd take on this skinny runt of a dog as well.

Would she take on…?

No. Or…way too soon.

Or way too stupid.

'You want her?' Henrietta was clearly delighted. She checked out Nick, clearly figuring if she could go for more. 'If Misty wants hers plus the whippet, and your little boy wants another, then we have plenty…'

'No,' Misty and Nick said as one, and then they grinned at each other. Grinning felt great, Nick thought. Even if it involved a whippet.

'Do you think she'll let me pick her up?' Bailey asked.

'Try her out, sweetheart,' Henrietta said and

Bailey scooped her up and the whippet licked his face like Ketchup had licked Misty's.

'There's been kids in these dogs' background,' Henrietta said, surveying the scene in satisfaction.

'And pizza,' Misty said. 'I bet this little girl likes pizza.'

'That means we need to have pizza tonight,' Bailey said. 'On the beach again. Or on the veranda. We're going to live together,' he told Henrietta. 'Can we take her, Dad?'

'I guess…'

'Then she's Took.'

'Took?' Nick said, bemused.

'Yes,' Bailey said in satisfaction, cuddling one scrawny dog and one battered teddy. But then he glanced along the row of dogs and looked momentarily subdued. 'But… Only one?'

'Only one.' That was Misty and Nick together again.

'Okay,' Bailey said, with a last regretful look at the rest of the inmates. He hugged his new dog closer, as if somehow loving this one could rub off on the rest. 'She's mine. I'm calling her Took 'cos that's what she is.' He smiled shyly up at Henrietta. 'Me and Dad and Ketchup and Took are going to live on both sides of Miss Lawrence's house and we're going to cut a hole in the wall.'

'Why not just open the door?' Henrietta said, and chuckled, and went to do the paperwork.

They took the two dogs back out to the farm and left them in the laundry while they shifted Nick and Bailey's gear.

That took less than an hour.

The laundry was shared by both sections of the house. In theory, they could put the dogs there to sleep. During the day Misty could take Ketchup to her side of the house and Bailey could take Took to his side. But it was never going to happen. Bailey was in and out of Misty's side about six times in the first fifteen minutes.

'I need to go see Gran,' Misty decreed at last, so both dogs settled in the sun on the veranda. Together. When Misty came home, both dogs and Nick and Bailey were on the veranda. Together.

Two days ago, this veranda had been all hers. Now…

Now she had emotions running every which way.

But why quibble? If she had to put her dreams on hold, maybe this was the next best thing.

They ate pizza again—'Just to show Took we can,' Bailey explained. Then Nick read his son a bedtime story on his side of the house and he came outside again as Misty was thinking she ought to go into her side of the house. But Took had left her now-sleeping owner and come back to join Ketchup. Both dogs were at her feet. Why disturb them?

Rockers on the veranda? Any minute now, Nick would offer to make her cocoa.

'Can I make you cocoa?' Nick asked and she choked.

'What?' he demanded.

'It needed only that.'

'It is…cosy,' he ventured and she grinned and shook her head.

'Ma and Pa and Kid and Dogs. It's not the image I want to take to bed with me.' She rose and picked up her dogs. Her *dog*, she reminded herself. And Bailey's dog. In time, they might teach Took to sleep on Bailey's bed. But she had a very clear idea of exactly what would happen. Ketchup and Took would both be on Bailey's bed. Two dogs on a child's bed…

It was the same as cocoa.

She'd settle them in the laundry and go do some

schoolwork, she told herself and turned to the
door. But Nick was before her, opening the door,
and then, as she struggled to keep Took's long
legs under control, he lifted Took from her and
followed her.

They'd set up two dog beds. They put a dog
in each, side by side. Ketchup whimpered and
Took sidled from her basket into Ketchup's. She
sort of sprawled her long legs around Ketchup so
Ketchup was wrapped in a cocoon of whippet.

'These guys are great,' Nick said, smiling and
rising, and Misty smiled and rose, too, only she
rose too fast and Nick was just…there.

His face was right by hers. His hands were
steadying her.

Back away fast.

She couldn't.

There was something between them she didn't
recognise. There'd been no guy in Banksia Bay
who made her feel…like she felt like she was
feeling now.

She didn't want him to let her go.

They were standing in her grandmother's
laundry. How romantic was that? The dogs were
snuffling at their feet. That was hardly romantic,
either.

She didn't feel romantic. She didn't feel…

She felt…

She was tying herself in knots. She had to step away, but his hold on her was tightening. He was looking down at her, his eyes questioning. If she tugged then he'd let her go. She knew it.

How could a girl tug?

She smiled up at him, a silly quavery smile that said she was being a fool. A sensible adult would step away and close the doors between them and treat this as just…as just him steadying her because she'd risen too fast.

But one of his hands had released her shoulder, and now his fingers were under her chin, tilting her face to meet his.

Yes.

No?

Um…yes. Yes, and yes and yes. Her face was definitely tilting and there was no need for his fingers to propel. She was propelling all by herself. Her bare toes were rising so she was on tiptoe, so he could hold her tighter, so she could meet…

His mouth.

Her whole world centred on his mouth.

Her lips parted involuntarily, and why wouldn't they? She was being kissed by a man who'd made her body melt practically the first time she'd seen him. *See a man across a crowded room and your world turns to fire...* She'd read that somewhere, in a romance novel or a short story or even a poem. She'd thought it was nuts.

Nicholas Holt had walked into her classroom and she'd thought he was Adonis. Only he wasn't. He was just...Nicholas.

He was pressuring her mouth to open, gently, wondrously, and her lips were responding. She seemed to be melting. Her mouth seemed to be merging with his. His hands were tugging her up to him. Her breasts were moulding to his chest. The world was dissolving into a mist of desire and wonder and white-hot heat.

He tasted of salt, of warmth, of wonder. He tasted of...

Nicholas.

Her body no longer belonged to her. It felt strange, different, as if she were flying.

She let her tongue explore his. Oh, the heat...

Oh, but he felt good.

'Misty...'

It was his voice, but she scarcely recognised it. He'd put her a little away from him and his voice was husky, with passion and with desire. He wanted her.

It felt powerful to be wanted by a man like this. It felt amazing.

'Mmm?' Their mouths were apart, but only just. She let her feet touch the floor again, grounding herself a little with bare toes on bare boards. Cooling off.

'It's too soon,' he whispered into her hair, but he didn't let her go.

'To take me to bed, you mean?' she whispered back and she surprised herself by managing a trace of laughter. 'Indeed it is. So if you think…'

'I'm not thinking.'

Only of course he was. They both knew what they were both thinking.

And why not? She was twenty-nine years old, Misty thought with sudden asperity. If they both wanted it…

Um…she'd known the guy for two days. He was right. It was too soon.

'So back on your side of the door, tenant,' she managed and he smiled and put her further away, but he was still holding her. They were a whole six inches apart but his hands were on her shoulders and if he tugged…

He wouldn't tug. They were both too sensible for that.

'Let's just see where this goes,' he said and she nodded.

'Yes.'

'But not tonight.'

'No.'

'So different doors?'

'Yes,' she said.

'And a small hole in the wall for dogs and Bailey. But not for us.'

'But rockers on the veranda?' she said, trying to smile.

'Not cocoa?' He was laughing at her.

'No!'

'Dangerous thing, cocoa.'

'It is,' she said with asperity. 'Even cocoa has risks.'

Risks. She thought suddenly, inexplicably, of her list. Her scrapbooks.

Her scrapbooks were dreams. Maybe fate had sent her Nicholas instead.

CHAPTER SEVEN

How could a girl sleep soundly after that? She managed a little, but she slept thinking Nick was just through the wall and she woke up thinking the same.

Nick was her tenant, but their worlds were already intertwined.

Was that a good thing?

Monday. School. No matter how muddled her thoughts, she needed to get going.

She went to check the dogs and found them already on the back lawn, with Nick supervising. He was wearing his boxers again, and nothing else. *Get dressed before you leave your side of the house,* she wanted to say, but she didn't because that'd tell him she'd noticed. And she didn't want to make a big deal of it.

Besides…she was absurdly aware that she wasn't dressed either, or she was, but just in her nightie that was a bit too short and her pink fluffy slippers that were just a bit too silly.

'Cute,' Nick said, surveying her from the toes up, and her toes were where her blush started.

'Inappropriate,' she said, flustered. 'Go get your son ready for school.'

'Yes, ma'am.' He hesitated and she felt like fleeing and finding a bathrobe.

She didn't have a bathrobe.

She'd buy one in her lunch hour this very day.

'If you take Bailey to school I'll look after the dogs,' he said.

'Okay,' she said cautiously, wondering what she was getting herself into. Suddenly she was committed to a school run? 'You'll need to pick him up, though,' she warned. 'I visit Gran after school.'

'Of course,' he said. 'The dogs can come with me.'

'They'll be okay by themselves if you need to leave.'

'Mostly I'll stay,' he told her. 'I have my desk set up overlooking the sea. My son's safe. I'll have dogs at my feet. What more could a man want?'

'A pipe and slippers,' she said, and she caught herself sounding waspish. What was wrong with a pipe and slippers?

'You'll need to think about shopping,' she told him. 'You can't live on pizza for ever.'

'Would you like to eat together tonight?'

'No!' It was a response of pure panic.

'No?'

'I...I may need to stay longer with Gran. Sometimes I grab a takeaway burger and eat with her.'

'Is she very ill?'

'She's not aware...' she started and then her voice trailed off at the impossibility of explaining the unexplainable. 'Or maybe she is. I'm not sure.'

'I'm sorry.'

'No, but sometimes I think she is. And then I stay.' She hesitated. 'Maybe she'd like to meet Bailey. I'll tell her about him. If you think Bailey...'

'We could do that,' he said gravely. 'Tell me when.'

When I'm ready, she thought as he retreated to his side of the house and closed the door behind him. When I'm ready to admit that these doors might stay open.

'That was fast.'

Playtime. She was on yard duty. Frank hardly

ever graced the grounds with his presence, but today the Principal of Banksia Bay Primary wandered out as she supervised play and nudged her, grinning with a leer she hated. 'I didn't think you had it in you.'

'What?' Frank could be obnoxious, and she suspected he was about to give a display.

'Nicholas Holt. Taking him home to bed already?'

Great. She might have known Frank would make it into a big deal. Most locals wouldn't think less of her for taking Nick and Bailey in as tenants, but the school Principal had a grubby mind.

'And you've got a dog,' Frank said. 'I thought you were clearing the decks.'

'What do you mean?'

'So you could get out of here after your grandmother dies.'

No one else would say it to her face, Misty thought. No one else was so horrible.

But she'd known Frank for a long time, and she was well past the stage where he could upset her. 'Leave it, Frank.'

'Don't do it, Mist.'

'Sorry?'

Suddenly Frank's voice was serious. Once upon a time she and Frank had been friends. He was the same age as she was. At fifteen…well, they hadn't dated but they'd hung out together and they'd shared dreams.

'I'm going to be a politician,' he'd said. 'I'll go to Canberra, do Political Science. I can make a difference, Mist.'

And then he'd fallen head over heels with Rebecca Steinway and Rebecca had eyes for only one thing—marriage and babies and not necessarily in that order. So, instead of going to Canberra, at eighteen Frank had become a father, struggling to do the same teacher's course Misty was doing.

Their qualifications were the same. Misty could have applied for the top teaching spot when it became vacant—she'd done a lot better in the course than Frank—but, by the time the old Principal had retired, Frank had three babies and was desperate for the extra money.

And now…

'You'll be stuck in this dump with a stepkid,' he said, almost roughly.

'I'm taking in tenants, not getting engaged. And it's not a dump. It's a great place…'

'To raise a family? Is that what you want?' Then he laughed and turned away. 'But of course it is,' he said. 'The only one who ever really wanted to get out of here was me. So much for your list, Misty. One dose of hormones and it's shot to pieces.'

She watched him go, his shoulders slumped. She didn't feel sorry for him, or not very. He could change what he was. Rebecca was nice, bubbly, cuddly. They had good kids. But staying here…being trapped…

It had changed him, destroyed something in him that was fundamental to who he was, she conceded. Frank was no longer faithful to Rebecca. He was no longer committed to this school.

Your list is fundamental to who you are, a voice whispered. *It's why you've got up in the morning for years.*

She closed her eyes. Her list wasn't important. Was it?

When she opened her eyes, Bailey was being towed to the sandpit by Natalie, the two of them giggling.

Bailey looked like his dad. Nicholas was gorgeous. Nicholas made her feel…

As Rebecca had once made Frank feel?

Stop it, she told herself harshly. Don't even go there. One day at a time, Misty Lawrence, and don't you dare pull back because of Frank, or a stupid, unattainable list. If you do, then you risk ending up with nothing.

But, decision or not, she didn't eat with them that night. Deliberately. Gran was more deeply asleep than usual when she visited her after school but she decided she'd stay on anyway. She did her schoolwork by Gran's bedside and at eight she finally went home.

Nick was on the veranda, by himself.

Her heart did this queer little twist at the sight of him. Stupid.

He wasn't by himself, she saw as she got nearer. The two dogs were at his feet and for some reason that made her heart twist all over again.

They looked up and wagged their tails and settled again.

'Is your gran okay?' Nick asked, and smiled, and her stupid heart did its stupid back flip with pike. Stop it, stop it, stop it.

'She's okay,' she managed. 'The dogs?'

'They've been missing you.'

'Really?' They'd done their tail wagging. Their eyes closed again. 'They're ecstatic to see me?'

'I'm ecstatic to see you.'

'At least they wagged their tails,' she retorted, deciding to treat that remark very lightly indeed.

'I don't do a good wag.'

'Neither do I. Especially when I'm tired.'

Was she tired? No, but it seemed the sensible thing to say. It was a precursor to walking right by him, going inside, closing the door.

'There's wine in my refrigerator,' he said, motioning to the glass in his hand. 'I'm only one glass down. It's good wine. I was hoping you'd join me.'

'I...' She gathered herself, her books, her resolution. 'Thank you, no. I need to do some work.'

'Really?'

'Really.'

'Scared, Misty?'

Scared? Maybe she was, but she wasn't admitting it. Last night's kiss had done things to her she didn't want to admit, even to herself. 'It's you who's scared of risks,' she managed.

'I'm not fearful here,' he told her. 'And I'm not

fearful for me. I'll do whatever it takes to make my son safe, and he's safe here.'

She didn't like that. The tiny sizzle inside her faded, cooled.

Last night's kiss had started something in her heart that she wasn't sure what to do with. There was a warmth, the promise of fire, the promise of things to come.

My son's safe here.

That was the statement of a man who loved his child above all else. As a teacher, she should have warmed to him saying it. She did.

But had last night's kiss been more of the same? Part of a strategy to make his son safe?

'I do need to work,' she said, trying desperately to tighten things inside that needed to be tightened. To sit on the veranda and drink wine with this man…to plan on doing it again tomorrow and the night after…

No. She would not be part of his safety strategy, or no more than she already was.

'Are the dogs okay?' she asked, managing to make her voice brisk.

'They're great,' he said. 'We carried Ketchup down to the beach after school. Took ran about ten miles in wider and wider circles until we all felt dizzy. Ketchup lay on the rug and watched Took and quivered all over. He'll be running in no time.'

She bit her lip. If she'd come straight home she could have joined them. Maybe Nick and Bailey had been expecting her to come home in time to join them.

It was just as well she hadn't. Be practical.

'They're fed?'

'They're both fed. Ketchup's had his painkillers and his antibiotics. Would you like to take him inside with you?'

She looked down at her dog. He was nestled at Nick's feet, warm against Took. Took was so thin; she needed Ketchup's body warmth. And Ketchup would still be hurting. With Took...

With Nicholas...

'They need each other,' she said. 'They're fine with you.'

'Ketchup's supposed to be your dog.'

'Yours, mine, this is just home.'

'My thoughts exactly,' Nick said and rose. 'Are you sure you don't want wine?'

'No.'

'Cocoa?'

'No!'

'That got a reaction,' he said, and grinned. 'You don't see yourself as a cocoa girl?'

'I have some living to do before then.'

'This is a great spot to do some living,' he said contentedly.

'No,' she said, and she remembered Frank's words. They weren't about her, she thought. It shouldn't matter that one man had been trapped and turned bitter.

But, oh, the bitterness…

'This might be a place for you to retreat to and live the rest of your life after danger,' she whispered, bending to give Ketchup a pat, a scratch behind his ears, before she made her escape. 'But for me it's a place to come home to between living.'

He frowned. 'What do you mean?'

'Meaning I've never had danger at all,' she told him. 'Not…not that I want it. Of course I don't. But I would have liked one little adventure before I retired to my rocker and cocoa.'

He was looking confused. As well he might, she thought. Her dreams were nothing to do with this man.

'Sorry, I'm being dumb,' she managed. 'But I do need to do some work. Enjoy your evening.' And she bolted through the screen door onto her side of the house before he could probe any more.

I've never had danger at all... What sort of stupid statement was that? But she knew what she meant.

'Your list is hopeless,' she whispered to herself as she closed the door on man and dogs. So stop rabbiting on about danger. About adventures.

Deep breath. 'Okay,' she told herself. 'Let's get this in perspective. Yes, I kissed him and yes, I liked it. Or more than liked it,' she conceded. 'But I won't be kissed because I'm a safe haven. Nicholas Holt and his son are gorgeous but I'm not stupid. At least—please don't let me be stupid. Please let me keep my head. Please don't let me turn into Frank.

'And please give me strength to stay on my side of the door.'

How could she live in the house and avoid him? She tried, but in the mornings when Bailey bounced through to be taken to school she couldn't miss him.

She dressed early now—there was no way he was catching her in her nightwear again—but even when she was ready for them...

Nick leaned his long body against the kitchen bench while she finished her coffee and Bailey gave her a full report on all that had happened since she'd last seen him.

Seeing that was only since school finished the night before, it was hardly momentous but there was still a lot to tell—how many seagulls Took had chased, or that Dad had cooked sausages for them the night before—she'd smelled them and it had almost killed her not to dump her pasta and head next door—and how Dad's sketches of his new boat were almost finished and it was going to be beeyootiful and it was going to be built in England but Dad said they couldn't go and see it.'

'Why not?' She couldn't help herself asking. She could be polite. She just couldn't be involved.

She was not a safe haven.

But it seemed she was, like it or not. 'This is where we live now,' Bailey said happily. He hesitated. 'Gran Rose and Papa Bill still live in England but Dad says they might come out and see us soon.'

'Isabelle's parents,' Nick explained.

'Dad's Mom and Papa don't like us very much,' Bailey confided. 'When I was in hospital they told Dad, "Reap as you sow". I don't exactly know what it means but Dad got angry and Gran Rose started to cry and then they went away. And they think Australia's dangerous.'

'Oh, dear,' Misty said and abandoned the rest of her coffee and bundled Bailey to school. Feeling ill for Nick.

Ill or not, she could not afford sympathy. It was important not to get caught up in his shadows.

Yeah, and pigs might fly but she didn't have to hang round the kitchen one minute longer than she must.

She didn't need to hang round Nicholas Holt.

She was not safe.

She arrived home the next night and Nick was in the laundry, inside her washing machine. Bits were spread everywhere. He was wearing greasy overalls and she couldn't see his head.

'So how long's it been taking itself on tours all over the laundry?' he asked, muffled by washing machine. 'And ripping the odd shirt.'

'I had someone look at it last week.' Indeed she had, and last month as well. 'Buy a new one,' the mechanic had said. 'It's well past its use-by date.'

Nick inflicted a couple of satisfactory thumps

and a final one for good measure before hauling himself out from underneath. 'I'm thinking she'll be right now,' he said. 'I just need to put her back together.'

There was a long line of grease running down the side of his nose. He had grease in his hair. He looked...he looked...

She didn't want to think how he looked.

He put the washing machine back together. It purred like a kitten. She and Bailey watched the first load in respectful awe.

Nick tried not to look smug. Misty thought she wouldn't need to use her list money to pay for a new washing machine. Misty thought there was a man in greasy overalls in her laundry.

She was having trouble not purring herself.

Which just went to show, she thought, as she retreated hastily to her side of the house.

She wasn't the least bit safe—and Nicholas Holt was starting to look downright dangerous.

'I don't want it to be the weekend.' Bailey announced to the world on Friday morning, and she wasn't surprised. Bailey had taken to school with joy, and the thought of no school tomorrow seemed more than Bailey could bear.

'You'll have the dogs to play with, and it'll do you good to sleep in,' Nick told his son, delivering him to Misty's kitchen for the ride to school. 'It'll do us all good. Miss Lawrence works too hard.'

Um…she didn't need to, Miss Lawrence admitted to herself. There wasn't a huge amount of correction to be done for Grade One, and she'd created so many lesson plans over the last few evenings she could rest on her laurels for a month.

But she wasn't about to admit that out loud. If only he wouldn't wear those jeans in her kitchen. If only he wouldn't lean against her bench. If only he'd stop fixing things. If only he'd stop smiling. If only he wasn't so long, so rangy. So… Nicholas

No.

'I work no harder than I must,' she said primly and bustled Bailey out to the car with speed, but she was aware of him watching her as she drove away.

He was amused?

He knew she was attracted to him, she thought. But did he know just how afraid she was? Of being kissed.

No. She wasn't the least afraid of being kissed.

She was afraid of being safe.

She was afraid, he thought, and he wasn't sure why. Had she been burned in the past? Roger Proudy and his sloppy kisses?

Why was it important to figure it out?

It wasn't important. It couldn't be important. He'd known Misty Lawrence for less than a week. He'd made an absolute commitment to his son, to do what he must to give him the stability he needed. That did not include getting involved with any woman.

Only this wasn't any woman. This was Misty and she made him feel…different.

Yeah, she was warm, funny, loving. She didn't threaten his plans for the future in any way—rather she augmented them.

But what he was feeling was more than that.

He was working on plans for a seriously large yacht. She was being built in England. He should be there now, but this new way—delegating responsibility to a partner—was working fine. He sat in the big front room with his plans spread out over two tables. He was consulting via Skype.

He could see what was happening every step of the way.

He should be excited by this project. He *was* excited, but undercutting his excitement was… Misty.

The vision of Misty was always there, in front of him.

The dogs were sleeping on his feet as he worked. Misty and Bailey were both at school. He should be knee-deep in boat plans.

He was, but…

'But tomorrow's Saturday,' he told the dogs. 'Tomorrow we get to take a day off. We'll all take a day off. Together?'

Separate houses. Separate lives.

He looked at the two dogs. Separate lives? Yeah, right. They'd figured it out.

Misty.

He needed to do a bit of figuring himself.

Saturday morning, and Misty had every intention in the world of keeping the door between the sides of the house firmly shut.

She could use some extra sleep, she told herself, so she didn't set her alarm, and when she heard a door slam and a child giggle on the other side of the house she closed her eyes again and wished she'd closed the curtains.

Only when had she ever? Her almost floor-length windows opened out to the veranda, to the sea. The breeze was making the net curtains flutter outward. It'd be a great day, Misty thought, and yawned and stretched—and a dog landed on her chest.

Any dog but Took might have winded her, but Took was a very slight dog and she barely packed a whumph.

'Yikes,' she said and Took quivered and licked. It was good to have dogs back here, she thought. It was great.

And more. Bailey's head poked though the window, peering around the net curtains. 'Took! Dad said we're not allowed to wake up Miss Lawrence.'

Took, it seemed, wasn't following instructions. She stood on Misty's chest and continued quivering, but not with fear. This was excitement.

So much for separate. Misty chuckled and moved sideways in the bed so Bailey could join them. Then she realised Ketchup was at the window, whining at being left out. With one gammy leg, he couldn't manage the twelve-inch sill, so she had to climb out of bed, scoop Ketchup up and scoot back to bed before anyone…anyone in particular…came looking for his son.

She tugged the covers to her chin. She was covered in two dogs and Bailey. She was respectable.

'Where's your father?' she asked, trying to sound…uninterested.

'In the shower. He takes ages. What will we do today?'

'I'm not sure what you're doing,' Misty said cautiously. 'This morning I'll visit my gran, and this afternoon I'm sailing.'

'Sailing.' Bailey lit with excitement. 'I like sailing. Can Dad and I come?'

'Come where?' And it was Nick—of course it was Nick—speaking from right outside the window. So much for showers taking ages. He did have the decency not to stick his head in, though. 'What are you two planning?'

'Sailing,' Bailey said and flew to the window to tug the curtains wide. 'Miss Lawrence and I are going sailing.'

Nick was wearing jeans again and a T-shirt, a bit too tight. His hair was wet. He looked… He looked…

Like it was totally inappropriate for him to be looking through her bedroom window.

At first glance he'd been smiling—his killer smile—but Bailey's words had driven the smile away.

'You're not sailing,' he told his son.

Misty thought that was his prerogative, but his voice was so hard, so definite, so unexpectedly angry that, before she could help herself, she heard herself say, 'Why not?'

'We don't sail.'

'You design yachts,' she said in astonishment. 'You built a yacht.'

'I design yachts, yes, but that's all. Bailey doesn't sail.' It was a grim snap, and somehow it was impossible not to respond.

'Says your mother.'

His face froze. Uh oh, she thought grimly. That was out of line. She'd overstepped the boundaries—of what was wise, of what was kind. This was not her business.

But she'd said it. The words hung. It was the second time she'd goaded him about his paranoia, and his smile wasn't coming back.

'I beg your pardon?' he said, icy with anger.

Should she apologise? Part of her said yes. The other part wasn't having a bar of it.

'Ooh, who's cross?' she ventured, thinking there was no unsaying what she'd said. It might even be a good thing that she had said it, she decided. Someone had to fight for Bailey. Maybe they should have this out when Bailey wasn't around, but Bailey looked interested rather than worried.

'Dad fusses,' he said and she nodded.

'I guess if I had a little boy who'd just come out of hospital I might fuss, too.' She peeped Bailey a conspiratorial smile, a smile of mischief. 'But the sailing I do is pussycat. I have a Sharpie, a tiny yacht, I'd guess it's far smaller than anything you guys have ever sailed. The bay's safe as houses. Bailey, if your dad lets you try *Mudlark* out—that's the name of my boat, by the way, because the first time I tried her out I got stuck in mud—we could stay in shallow water. And of course we'd wear life vests.'

'You got stuck in mud?' Bailey said, entranced.

'It was very embarrassing,' she told him. 'Philip Dexter, the town's lawyer, had to tow me off. I'm a better sailor now.'

'Dad...' Bailey said.

'No,' Nick said, refusing to be deflected.

'I can swim,' Bailey said, jutting his jaw at his father. They really were amazingly alike.

'No.'

'I'll wear a life vest.'

'Life vests are great,' Misty said. 'They take all the worry out of tipping over.'

'You tip over?' Bailey said, casting a dubious glance at his father.

'Sometimes,' she admitted, being honest. In truth, there was nothing she loved more than setting her little boat into the wind, riding out conditions that had more experienced yachtsmen retire to the clubhouse. Tipping was part of the fun. 'But today's really calm—not a tipping day at all. If your dad did decide to let you come I'd be very careful.'

She ventured a cautious peek at Nick then and thought, *Uh oh*. She wasn't making headway. Nick looked close to explosion. But if he was about to explode...Why not take it all the way?

'You know, if your father was on board, too...' she ventured. 'I'm thinking your dad knows yachts better than I do. I bet he'd never let it tip over.'

'No!' Nick said, and it was a blast of pure icy rage.

Should she leave it? She glanced at Bailey and she thought Nick had brought him here, to this house, because he thought it was safe. Because he thought she was safe.

And something inside her matched his fury. She was *not* going to stick to his rules.

'So what else do you intend to forbid?' she demanded. 'Every kid in Banksia Bay plays in a boat of some sort. Canoes, dinghies, sailboards, surf-kites, water-skis. This is a harbour town.'

'Will you butt out?'

'No,' she said. 'Not when you're being ridiculous.'

'Ridiculous,' Bailey said and finally—and probably too late—Misty decided she'd gone too far. Nick's face was almost rigid. His own child calling him ridiculous…

A woman might just have to back off.

'Maybe your dad's right,' she told Bailey, and she hugged him against her. She was still in bed, with Bailey and dogs crowded in with her. Nick seemed suddenly an outsider.

She looked at his face and she saw pain behind his anger. Worse, she saw fear. He'd been to hell and back over the last year, she thought. What was she doing, adding to it because she was angry?

'Maybe ridiculous is the wrong word,' she conceded. 'Maybe I'm not being fair. Your dad worries because of what happened to you and your mum, because he knows bad things happen. He brought you to Banksia Bay because it's safe, and it is, but maybe he needs time to see it. I tell you what; why don't you and your dad bring the dogs to the beach this afternoon and watch? When your dad sees how safe it is, then maybe next Saturday or the one after that he'll agree.'

'You think I'm being dumb,' Nick said, sounding goaded.

'I do.' She hugged the dogs and she hugged Bailey. 'But that's your right.'

'Being dumb.'

'Being…safe. But let's change the subject,' she said—and the frustration in his eyes said it was high time she did. 'You and Bailey talk about sailing and let me know if you ever want to join me. Meanwhile, I need to go see Gran. So if you gentlemen could give me a little privacy and if you could take the dogs with you it would be appreciated,' she said, and she smiled at Nick and she kept her smile in place until he'd taken his son and their dogs and let her be.

'Why not?' Bailey demanded as soon as Misty's door was shut.

'If anything happened to your arm...'

He was talking to a six-year-old. He should just say no and be done with it. What happened to the good old days when a man was master in his own home?

This was Misty's home. Her rules?

'I can wear my brace,' Bailey said, and he slid his hand into his father's. Beguiling as only a six-year-old could be.

'No.'

'Dad...'

'We'll think about it. Later.'

'Okay,' Bailey said. He really was a good kid. There'd been so many things he couldn't do over the last year that he was used to it. 'Can we make Ketchup and Took bacon for breakfast?'

'Yes,'

'Hooray,' Bailey said and sped away, dogs in pursuit.

How much bacon did he have? Enough for dogs?

He could borrow some from Misty.

The way he was feeling… No.

But then he thought of Misty, her chin tilted, defiant, pushing him to the limit.

And he thought of his son.

There'd been so many things Bailey couldn't do over the last year…

What was he doing, adding more?

Define *safe*, he thought, and he thought of Misty in bed with dogs and Bailey.

Misty was safe.

Misty was gorgeous.

The feeling stilled and settled.

Misty was home.

CHAPTER EIGHT

MISTY visited Gran, who was so deeply asleep she couldn't be roused.

Discomfited, worrying about Gran and worrying almost as much about the guys she'd left at home, she made her way to the yacht club. There was no need for her to go home to change. She kept her gear here.

'Hey, Misty, how's the boyfriend?' someone called, and there was a general chuckle.

She didn't flush. She didn't need to, for the words had been a joke. But inside the joke made her flinch. Was it so funny to think Misty could ever have a boyfriend?

It had been four years since she'd had any sort of relationship, she thought, as she fetched her sailing clothes from her locker. She'd been twenty-five. Luke had been her friend from kindergarten. He'd been away to the city, broken his heart and come home to Misty. He'd wanted to marry, settle on his parents' farm and breed babies and cows.

She'd knocked him back. He'd married Laura Buchanan and they had two babies already and four hundred Aberdeen Angus.

Since then… Misty was twenty-nine and for four years she'd lived alone with her scrapbooks and a list. Miss Havisham in the making?

'What's he like?' someone called, and she tugged herself back to the here and now. 'The boyfriend.'

'Wildly romantic,' she threw back, figuring she might as well go along with it. 'I've seen him in his pyjamas. Sexy as.'

She hadn't seen him in his pyjamas. She'd seen him in his boxers. He was indeed sexy.

Let's not go there.

'Woohoo,' someone called. 'Our Misty has a life!'

Only she hadn't. She changed into her yachting gear and the old frustrations surged back.

Nick had kissed her. *Misty has a life?* Maybe she had. If she wanted it, a relationship was beckoning.

But why had he kissed her? He was attracted to her because she was Misty, the safe one.

Luke had broken his heart and come back to her.

To Misty. To safe.

She glanced out at the bay and saw a gentle breeze rippling the water. It was perfect sailing conditions, but she didn't want perfect. She wanted twenty-foot waves, a howling sou-easterly and trouble.

'My turn to win this time,' someone said and it was Di, the local newsagent. At sixty-five, Di was still one of the town's best sailors. She'd represented Australia in the Olympics. She'd travelled around the world honing her skills.

Misty had stayed home and honed hers.

She and Di were competitive enough. In this bay she could often beat her. But if she ever got out of this bay…

Who knew? She certainly didn't.

Don't think about it, she told herself. Concentrate on beating Di.

And not thinking about Nick?

The race didn't start until two. Mostly the yachties sat round the clubhouse talking, but Misty bought a sandwich and launched *Mudlark*. She sailed out to the entrance to the bay—looking for trouble? But conditions outside weren't any different to inside.

No risks today. Safe as houses.

What was wrong with safe? she demanded of herself. Get over it.

Thoroughly unsettled, she sailed her little boat back inside and spent an hour practising, pushing herself so she had *Mudlark* so tuned to the wind she was flying.

Finally, it was time to make her way to the start line. She'd win today.

There was nothing else to aim for.

Oh, for heaven's sake, what was wrong with her? If Gran could hear her now she'd give her a tongue-lashing. What was the point of complaining about something you couldn't change?

What was wrong with settling for dogs and a lovely tenant—a tenant who'd kissed her…?

The boats were tacking backwards and forwards behind the starting line, trying to gain an edge. There were up to thirty Sharpies who raced each week. The yacht club kept some available for hire, so visitors to the town could join in. That made it more fun; often an out of town yachtie could surprise them. But no out of town yachtie could beat them.

Di had the experience. Misty had the local knowledge. It was Di or Misty, almost every week.

She checked Di's boat. Di was geared up, ready to go.

The starter's gun fired. *Mudlark* flew, streaming across the water, her sails catching the wind at just the right angle.

The wind was in her hair, on her face. She was sailing fast and free. If she couldn't have her list, this was the next best thing.

And Nick? Was he the next best thing?

A boat was edging up on the same tack as *Mudlark*. She saw it out of the corner of her eye and was surprised. She'd expected to be well in front by now.

And then… Startled, she realised it wasn't Di. It was one of the little orange Rentaboats.

Hey, an out-of-towner pushing her. That'd do to keep her mind off things. She tightened the jib, read the wind, tightened still more.

She passed the marker buoy. Brought her round. The Rentaboat was closing in. What the…?

No matter. Just win. Tug those sails in. Go.

Rentaboat was almost to the buoy and, as she

caught the wind and sailed back, she passed within ten yards.

'Hey, Miss Lawrence, we're racing you.' The high, excited yell pierced her concentration and Misty came close to letting go of her stays.

Bailey.

Nick.

'Go faster, Dad, we're catching up,' Bailey yelled and Misty saw Nick grin.

Her heart did this stupid crazy leap.

Nick was racing. Nick and Bailey…

Bailey was crouched in the bow, whooping with excitement, bright with life and wonder. Nick was at the helm, intent, a sailor through and through.

'Miss Lawrence!' Bailey yelled across the water. 'Miss Lawrence, we're going to win.'

Maybe they would. Her jib had slackened. She was tightening, tightening. Of all the…

She and Di were competitors with each other. Occasionally something happened and another local took line honours, but to concede honours to a Rentaboat…

Pride was at stake here.

She tuned and tuned, every sense totally focused on the boat, the water, the wind. But no, that was a lie because overriding everything else was the awareness that Nick was in the next boat.

He'd brought his son sailing.

A risk…

Hardly a risk. They were both wearing life vests; of course they were. They'd not be allowed to race without them. They were surrounded by a fleet of small boats. Even if they capsized, they'd be scooped up so fast there was never a hint of risk

But still…it was a start, Misty thought.

No, she corrected herself. Getting Took had been a start. This was simply the next step.

As finding Ketchup had been her start. Her start of retreating from her list, from her dreams.

What was her next step?

The wind rose, just a little. She should have seen it coming. Maybe she had seen it, but she was away with her lists. The sudden gust caught her unaware, pushed her sideways, dropped her speed.

Nick surged ahead.

'Hurray, we're winning,' Bailey yelled and they would; the finish line was in sight. But then…

Di. Misty hadn't even noticed her coming up

on the far side of Nick. Di's Sandpiper edged just ahead. Nosing over the line.

Local pride was intact. Di first. Nick and Bailey second.

Misty third.

But a win had never felt as good. It felt fantastic. It was as if she'd been granted the world.

Was it silly to feel like this?

Thoroughly disconcerted, she reduced sail, manoeuvred her little boat back to dock and was inordinately pleased to see Nick had trouble. You needed to know the currents around the clubhouse to get in tight. He didn't know the currents and was having to take an extra run.

Di was calling to him, congratulating him over the water. On the dock, Fred, the vet, was watching. Fred's son sailed. Fred usually watched his son but he was watching Nick now, and she remembered Fred's reaction when he'd heard Nick was a painter.

Nick would be painting for Fred's beloved repertory society in no time.

He'd be a local.

That was great. Wasn't it?

Befuddled, conflicted, she pushed her little boat into shore, then tugged her out onto the hard.

Nick needed to go further along, to return his Rentaboat. It gave her time to get her thoughts together, so when Bailey came hurtling through the yard gates and whooped towards her she could laugh and swoop him up into her arms and hug him. And smile over his shoulder to his father.

'You beat me.'

'Your mind must have been on other things,' he said, smiling back, and he looked...fantastic. Faded sweatshirt. Jeans rolled up to his knees. Strong, bare legs. Bare feet. Wind-tousled hair.

He was smiling straight into her eyes, and something was catching in her chest.

Your mind must have been on other things. Really? What could they have been?

'We should have warned you,' he said, and she wondered if she was blushing. She felt as if she was blushing. Was it showing? 'I believe Bailey's yell might have distracted you.'

'You really can sail,' she managed.

'It's what I do,' he said softly. 'It's what I love. I just...needed reminding.'

'That it's safe.'

'That it's still possible to have fun. We've forgotten a bit.'

'And now you have a dog and a sailing club,'

she said, a bit more sharply than she intended, and then wondered why she'd snapped. What was wrong with her? She should be pleased for him. She *was* pleased for him. She was delighted that he was starting to loosen up, become part of this community.

But there was something still not right. Something...

'Speaking of dogs... Did you leave them home?'

'What a question,' he said, sounding affronted. He motioned to the clubhouse yard. The dogs were tied under a spreading eucalypt, a water bowl in reach. They were occupied with a bone apiece. A vast bone apiece.

'I didn't do the bones,' he told her. 'But Fred told everyone their story within two minutes of them arriving and your local butcher headed straight back to his shop and brought them one each. Have you ever seen anything happier?'

She hadn't. She felt herself smiling. But then... Tears?

Of all the stupid, emotional...

She did not cry. She didn't. But now...

Dogs with happy endings. Nick and Bailey with happy endings.

And Nick was watching her. Mortification plus. But he wasn't laughing at her. He didn't look like her tears embarrassed him. He lifted his hand and he wiped a tear away before it had the chance to roll down her cheek.

His touch burned. She wanted to catch his hand and hold it against her face—just hold it.

People were watching.

What did it matter? Was this the next step?

'Hey, Nicholas…'

The moment—the danger?—had passed. Fred was bearing down on them, intentions obvious. 'Great sail. Well done. I hear you can paint.'

'Paint?' Nick said cautiously and Misty managed a chuckle as she moved swiftly away.

'Welcome to my world,' she murmured and went to congratulate Di. She hadn't taken his hand, she told herself. She'd stayed self-contained. Good.

But self-contained wasn't actually going to happen. Not if Bailey could help it. She'd taken two steps when he slid his hand into hers.

'When we go home can I come in your car? Dad says we can have fish and chips for tea. Can we eat tea together? The dogs and I would really like it.'

* * *

It seemed surly to refuse, so yes, they ate fish and chips together on the beach. Took bounded a mile or more and then settled beside Ketchup in blissful peace. Apart from looking enquiringly to the chips every now and then, both dogs seemed happy.

Ketchup was looking better every day. The initial pinning of the badly fractured leg needed follow-up. There'd be more surgery later on, but for now he was with Took and he'd found a home.

More, he'd found a boy. And boy had found dogs. The three of them were curing each other, Misty thought, as she watched Bailey tease Took with a chip—tease her, tease her, then shriek as Ketchup whipped in from the side to snatch it. While Bailey was expounding indignation, Took wolfed three more.

Bailey giggled, his father chuckled, Misty went to move the chips out of dog range, Nick did the same and somehow Nick's hand was touching hers again.

They glanced at each other. Nick moved the chips. Then he returned to touch again.

And hold.

'It's been a magical day,' he said softly. 'Thanks to Misty.'

'Thanks to Misty not winning, you mean,' she said with what she hoped was dry humour, but he shook his head and suddenly he had both her hands and he was drawing her closer.

'That's not what I mean at all. Misty…'

What was he doing? Was he planning to kiss her? Now?

'Not in front of Bailey,' she breathed. No!

'Not what in front of Bailey?' Nick asked, smiling down into her eyes. 'Not thanking his teacher for giving us a lesson in life?'

'How can I have done that?'

'Easy,' he said. 'By being you.' He tugged her closer. 'Misty…'

'No.'

'You mean you don't want me to kiss you?'

'No!'

The laughter was back in his eyes. Laughter should never leave him for long, she thought. He was meant for smiling.

He was meant for smiling at her?

'You mean no, you don't not want me to kiss you?' he asked, his smile widening. Becoming wicked.

'No!' She had to think of something more intelligent to say. She couldn't think of anything but Nick's smile.

'It's very convoluted,' he complained. 'I'm not sure I get it. So if I pulled you closer...'

'Nick...'

'Bailey, close your eyes,' he said. 'I need to give Miss Lawrence a thank you kiss.'

'She doesn't like 'em slurpy,' Bailey said wisely. 'She tells Ketchup that all the time.'

'Not slurpy,' Nick said. 'Got it.'

'And she hates tongues touching,' he added. 'That happened yesterday after Ketchup chewed the liver treat. She went and washed her mouth out with soap.'

'So no tongue kissing—or no liver treats?'

'Nick...' She was trying to tug away. She was trying to be serious. But his eyes were laughing, full of devilry, daring her. Loving her?

'Miss Lawrence has said I mustn't kiss her in front of you,' Nick told his son, and his eyes weren't leaving hers. He was making love to her with his eyes, she thought. How did that happen?

'I mean it,' she whispered.

'So can you take Took down and feed the rest of the chips to the seagulls?'

'Why? It's okay to watch.'

'What would the kids at school say if they saw you kissing a girl?' his father asked.

Bailey considered. 'I guess they'd giggle. And Natalie would say, "Kissie kissie". I think.'

'Exactly,' his father said. 'Miss Lawrence is really scared of giggling and she's even more scared of kissie kissie. So, unless you go away, I can't kiss her.'

'You can't kiss me anyway,' Misty managed and his eyes suddenly lost their laughter.

'Really?'

And how was a girl to respond to that?

'I don't...'

'Know?' he said. 'There's only one answer to that. Bailey, down to the water right now or there's no fish and chips on the beach until the next blue moon. Right?' And then, as Bailey giggled, and he and his dog headed towards the seagulls on the shoreline, he pulled her closer still. 'Ready or not...'

And he kissed her.

Second kiss.

Better.

He knew what he wanted.

His parents considered him insane for being a risk-taker. He'd sworn risk-taking would end.

Was it a risk to believe he was falling in love in little more than a week? Was it a risk to want this woman?

It had been a risk to think he was in love with Isabelle. More—it had been calamity. But this was no risk.

This was Misty. A safe harbour after the storm. A woman to come home to.

She wasn't pulling back. Her lips would feel warm, he thought. Full and generous. Loving and reassuring.

But then his mouth met hers and instead of warmth there was…more. Sizzle. Heat. Want.

Instead of kissing her, he found he was being kissed.

There was nothing safe about this kiss. It asked much more than it told, but it told so much. It told that this woman wanted him, ached for him, came alive at his touch.

It told him that she wanted him as much as he wanted her—and more.

Just a kiss…

Not just a kiss. He was holding a woman in his

arms and he was making her feel loved, desired. He knew it because the same thing was happening to him. The awfulness of the last twelve months was slipping away. More—the pain of a failing marriage, the knowledge that he was always walking a tightrope, slipped and faded to nothing, and all there was left was Misty.

He was deepening the kiss and she was as hungry as he was, as desperate to be close. Her hands tugged him closer. Closer still… She was moulding to him and her breathing was almost like part of him.

He wanted her so much…

He was on the beach with two dogs and his son.

Ketchup was nosing between them. Misty's hands were…pushing? She wanted to stop?

They should stop.

Who moved first? He didn't know; all he knew was that they were somehow apart and Misty was looking at him with eyes that were dazed, confused, lost.

'Misty…' Her look touched something deep within. Was she afraid?

She'd wanted him as much as he wanted her. Hadn't she?

Her look changed, the smile returned, but he knew he'd seen it.

'What is it?' he asked, but her smile settled back to the confidence, the certainty he knew. The impudent teasing that he somehow suspected was a mask.

'Entirely inappropriate, that's what it is,' she retorted. 'For me to kiss the parent of one of my students.'

Her student was whooping back to them now, trying to beat Took, who was practically dawdling. 'Can I come back now?' Bailey demanded.

'Yes,' Nick told him. 'And you're not to tell anyone.' His eyes didn't leave Misty's. 'That I kissed Miss Lawrence.'

'Why not?'

'People will tease us,' Nick said and Bailey considered and decided the explanation was reasonable.

'Like saying "kissie kissie".'

'Exactly. And then I wouldn't be able to kiss Miss Lawrence again.'

'I think you need to call me Misty,' she said, no longer looking at him. 'Bailey, when we're on our own, would you call me Misty? Could you re-member to call me Miss Lawrence at school?'

'Sure,' Bailey said. 'Do you think you'll marry Dad?'

What sort of question was that?

It was a reminder that fantasy had gone far enough. It was time for reality to kick in.

'Um…no,' Misty managed and the school-teacher part of her took charge. 'Kissing someone doesn't mean you have to marry them.'

'But it means you like them.'

'Yes,' she admitted, carefully not looking at him. She could feel colour surge from her toes to the tips of her ears. 'But I gave you a kiss goodnight last night. That doesn't mean I'll marry you.'

'It wasn't a kiss like the one you gave Dad.' Bailey sounded satisfied, like things were going according to plan. She cast him a suspicious look—and then turned the same one on his father.

'Have you guys been discussing kissing me?'

'No,' Nick said, but the way he looked…

'Has your father said he wants to kiss me?' she demanded of Bailey and Bailey looked cautiously at his father and then at Misty. Truth and loyalty were wavering.

'I'm your teacher,' Misty said, hauling her blush under control enough to sound stern. 'You don't tell fibs to your teacher.'

'Dad just told you a fib,' Bailey confessed, virtuous.

'Hey,' Nick said. 'Bailey…'

'So you have been talking about me?'

'I saw you kissing in the laundry,' Bailey said. 'I was sort of…up. But I hardly looked.' He grinned. 'But I saw Dad kiss you and later I asked if it was nice to kiss a girl and he said it depends on the girl. And then he said it was very, very nice to kiss you. So I asked if he was going to kiss you again and he said as soon as he possibly can. And tonight he did. Dad, was it okay?'

'Yes,' said Nick.

Misty glared at him. 'You planned…'

'I merely took advantage of an opportunity,' Nick said, trying to look innocent. 'What's wrong with that?'

'How many times do you have to kiss each other before you get married?' Bailey asked.

'Hundreds,' Misty said and then, at the gleam of laughter in Nick's eyes, she added a fast rejoinder.

'So that's why I'm never kissing your father again.'

'Really?' Nick asked and suddenly the laughter was gone.

'R…really.'

'It wasn't just a kiss,' he said softly. 'You know it was much more.'

'It was just a kiss. I'm your landlady.'

'I'm not asking for a reduction in the rent.'

'I'm thinking of putting it up.' She started clearing things, trying to be busy, doing anything but look at him.

'Why the fear?' Nick asked and she shook her head.

'No fear. You're the one who wants to be safe.'

'Hey, we went sailing.'

'I won't be safe,' she muttered.

He frowned. 'What sort of statement is that?'

'Safe as Houses Misty. That's me. Didn't you know? Isn't that why you kissed me? Now, if you'll excuse me, I need to go say goodnight to Gran.'

He was questioning her with his eyes, gently probing parts of her she had no intention of exposing. 'Misty, your Gran's been in a coma for months.'

'And I still need to say goodnight to her,' she snapped.

'Of course. I'm sorry. I'd never imply otherwise. You love her. It's one of the things…'

'Don't,' she said, panicking. 'Nick, please, don't. I need to go.'

'It wasn't just a kiss, Misty,' he said gently, and he rose and took the picnic basket from her and set it down on the sand before she could object. 'Was it?'

And there was only one answer to that. 'No.'

'Then let's not get our knickers in a knot,' he said and his sexy, seductive, heart-stopping smile was back. It was crooked, twisted and gorgeous, as if he was mocking, but there was no mocking about it. His smile was real and wonderful and it turned her knees to jelly.

'Bailey's going too fast for us,' he said. 'There's no rush. There's no need to panic. But still, it wasn't just a kiss. We both know it.' He took her hands and tugged her to him, only he didn't kiss her this time, at least not properly. He kissed her lightly on the tip of her nose.

'Let's take this slowly,' he said. 'We won't mess

this up by rushing. But maybe we both know it could be something wonderful. If we play it right— it could be home for both of us.'

Misty took the dogs with her because she wanted to talk to someone. She left Nick and Bailey sitting on the beach, and they had the sense to let her be.

As they should.

'Because they're my tenants,' she told Ketchup as she carried him. 'I need to be separate.'

But Took was bouncing along beside her. Took was Bailey's dog. Ketchup was her dog.

To separate the two would be cruel.

It felt a little like that now. She was aware of Nick and Bailey watching as she walked away. She was leaving Nick. She was leaving his laughing eyes, his sudden flashes of intuitive sympathy, his sheer arrant sexiness.

'See, that's what I can't resist,' she told Ketchup as she changed out of her sandy clothes to go to the hospital. 'He makes my toes curl but he just thinks I'm safe. If I give into him…if I dissolve like he wants me to dissolve, then I get to stay here for ever. In this house. Mother to Bailey.'

Wife to Nick?

'Maybe I want that,' she said. Ketchup was lying on her bed watching her while Took roamed the bedroom looking for anything deserving of a good sniff. 'Banksia Bay's fabulous, and so's this house. It's the best place in the world.'

As if in response, Took leaped onto the bed and curled up beside Ketchup. Misty looked down at them. Her two dogs, curled on her bed, happy, hopefully for the rest of their lives.

But… There was a scar running the length of Took's face from an unknown awfulness. Ketchup's leg was fixed tight in its brace.

'You guys have had adventures,' she whispered. 'Now you've come home, but I've never left.'

Don't think about it, she told herself. Take your scrapbooks and burn them.

Nicholas had kissed her and he'd touched something deep within. To risk losing what he promised…

For scrapbooks?

The kiss had felt amazing. Her body had responded in ways she'd never felt before.

'I'm a lucky girl,' she told the dogs. 'Yes, I should burn the scrapbooks.'

But she didn't. She slung her bag over her shoulder and she went to see Gran instead.

* * *

'Do you want to marry Misty?'

Nick had left enough time for Misty to change and go to the hospital. He was aware he was rushing things. Risking things. Now Bailey tucked his hand into his father's as they set off towards the house and he asked his most important question.

Did he want to marry Misty?

'I've already been married,' he said cautiously. 'It was dreadful when Mama was killed. It takes time for a man to be ready to marry again.'

'Yeah, but we sailed again.'

'So we did.'

'And it was awesome.'

'It was.'

'You marrying Misty would be awesome.'

Would it?

It wasn't his head telling him yes. It was every nerve in his body.

But he wouldn't rush it. He couldn't rush it. There were things he didn't understand.

She didn't want safe?

She must. To come home… He longed for it with all his heart.

And to come home to Misty…

Home and Misty. More and more, the images merged to become the same thing.

CHAPTER NINE

How had they become a couple in the eyes of the town? It had just…happened. There was little gossip, no snide rumours of the Frank variety. There was simply acceptance of the fact that Nick was sharing Misty's house, he was an eligible widower and Bailey needed a mother.

'And he's rich!' Louise, the Grade Five teacher, did an Internet search and discovered a great deal more information than Misty knew. 'He can demand whatever he wants for his designs,' she informed Misty, awed. 'People are queueing for him to work for them. If I'd realised what we had here I'd have kicked Dan and the kids out of the house and invited him home myself. You're so lucky.'

That was the consensus. Misty was popular in the town. A lonely childhood with two ailing, elderly grandparents made the locals regard her with sympathy. They knew of her dream to travel, and they knew she couldn't. This seemed a wonderful solution.

Especially since Nick was just...there. Wherever Misty was.

'So tell me what sort of steak you like for dinner,' he'd ask as he collected Bailey from school, making no secret of the fact that they were eating together. Well, why wouldn't they? The dogs and Bailey insisted the door dividing the house stayed open. Nick was enjoying cooking— 'Something I've never been able to try'—and it seemed churlish to eat TV dinners while the most tantalizing smells drifted from the other side.

They settled into a routine. After dinner they'd take the dogs to the beach. They carried Ketchup to the hard sand, set him down, and he sniffed the smells and limped a little way while Bailey and Took bounced and whooped around him.

Then Nick put Bailey to bed while Misty went back to say goodnight to Gran—whose sleep seemed to be growing deeper and deeper—and when she came home Nick was always on the veranda watching for her.

He worked solidly through the day—she knew he did for he showed her his plans—but he always put his work aside to wait for her. So she'd turn into the drive and Nick would be in his rocker, beer in hand. The dogs were on the steps. Bailey was sleeping just beyond.

It was seductive in its sweetness. Like the call of the siren…

Sometimes she'd resist. She did have work to do. When that happened Nick simply smiled and let her go. But, more and more, she'd weaken and sit on the veranda with him. No, she didn't drink cocoa but it was a near thing. He'd talk about the boat he was working on. He'd ask about her day. And then…as the night stretched out, maybe he'd mention a place he'd been to and she couldn't help but ask for details. So he'd tell her. Things he'd done. Places he'd been.

She was living her adventures vicariously, she thought. Nick had had adventures for her.

And then the moon would rise over the horizon and she'd realise the time and she'd rise…

And he'd rise with her and always, now, he'd kiss her. That was okay, for kissing Nick was starting to seem as natural as breathing. It seemed right and wonderful—and after a month she thought it seemed as if he'd always been a part of her life. And part of Banksia Bay.

He was painting for the repertory society. He

was repairing the lifeboat at the yacht club. He was making friends all over town.

And her friends were starting to plan her future.

'You know Doreen's mother's coming from England next term,' Louise said thoughtfully one school lunchtime. 'Doreen would love to get a bit of casual teaching while her mum's here to mind the kids. If you and Nick were wondering when to take a honeymoon...'

Whoa. She tossed a chalkboard duster at Louise. Louise ducked and laughed but Misty suspected she'd go away and plant the same idea in Nick's head.

So what? She should be pleased. Nick warmed parts of her she hadn't known were cold. He held her and he made her feel every inch a woman.

She should embrace this new direction with everything she possessed. She knew she should.

But then Nick would tell her about watching the sunset over the Sahara, or Bailey would say, 'You remember that humungous waterfall we walked under where there was a whole room behind?'

Or Nick would see a picture in the paper and say, 'Bailey, do you remember this? Your mother and I took you there...'

And she'd wait until they'd gone to bed and she'd check the Internet and see what they'd been referring to. The dogs would lie on her feet, a wonderful warm comfort, like a hot-water bottle. Loving her. Holding her safe.

Holding her here.

'So when do you think he'll pop the question?' Louise demanded as term end grew closer, and she blushed and said,

'He hasn't even...I mean we're not...'

'You mean you haven't slept with him yet?' Her friend threw up her hands in mock horror. 'What's keeping you, girl?'

Nothing. Everything. Louise got another duster thrown at her and Misty went to lay the situation before Gran.

'I love him,' she told Gran and wondered why it didn't feel as splendid as it sounded.

Maybe it was sadness that was making her feel ambivalent about this wonderful direction her life was taking. For Gran didn't respond; there was no longer any way she could pretend she did. Her hands didn't move now when Ketchup lay on the bed. There was no response at all.

Oh, Gran...

If she didn't have Nick...

But she did have Nick. She'd go home from

the hospital and Nick would hold her, knowing intuitively that things were bad. She'd sink into his embrace and he'd hold her for as long as she needed to be held. He'd kiss her, deeply, lovingly, but he never pushed. He'd prop her into a rocker and make her dinner and threaten her with cocoa if she didn't eat it.

He and Bailey would make her smile again.

What more could a girl want?

'Are you sure he hasn't asked?' Louise demanded a week later.

She shook her head, exasperated. 'No.'

'He looks like a man who's proposed. And been accepted.'

'How could I miss a proposal?'

'You're not encouraging him.' Louise glared. 'Get proactive. Jump his bones. Get pregnant!'

'Oi!'

'He's a hot-blooded male. There must be something holding him back.'

She knew there was. It was her reluctance. He sensed it and he wouldn't push.

All she had to do was smile. All she had to do was accept what he was offering.

She would, she thought. She must.

And then Gran…

* * *

Five in the morning was the witching hour, the hour when defences were down, when everything seemed at its worst. For some reason she woke. She felt strange. Empty.

Something was wrong. She threw back the covers and the phone rang.

Gran.

'She's dead.' She barely knew if she'd said it out loud. She was in the hall, standing by the phone, staring at nothing. And then Nick was there, holding her, kissing her hair, just holding.

'I…I need to go.'

'Of course you do. Put something warm on,' he said, and while she dressed—her fingers didn't work so well—she heard him on the phone. Then someone was at the front door. There was a short bark from Ketchup, quickly silenced, and she went out to find Louise in the hall.

Louise's husband farmed the neighbouring property, and Louise's son was in the same grade as Bailey. Louise and Misty often swapped classes, so Bailey already knew Louise well.

She hugged Misty now, tight. 'Oh, Misty, love, she was a lovely lady, your gran, she'll be missed.

Nick says he's going to the hospital with you, so we've agreed that I'll stay here until Bailey wakes. Then I'll scoop him home with me. Is it okay if I tell him what's happened?'

'It's okay,' she said numbly.

'And it's Saturday so there's no pressure,' Louise said. 'If Bailey's okay with it, maybe he can have a sleepover. That'll leave you to get on with things. But we can talk later. You'll be wanting to get to the hospital. Give her a kiss goodbye from me,' she told Misty and she hugged her again and propelled her out of the door.

Nick held her as they walked to the car. She shivered in the dark and moved closer. She'd known this was coming. It wasn't a shock. But...

'She's all I've had for so long.'

'I wish I'd met her,' Nick said. 'Your gran raised you to be who you are. She must have been wonderful.'

She huddled into the passenger seat while Nick drove and she thought of his words. They were a comfort.

And Nick had known Gran. He lived in Gran's house. He walked on the beach Gran loved. He cooked from her recipe books. And once... She'd needed to stay back late at school. It had been late before she'd made it to the hospital—something she hated. Gran probably no longer knew she came every day but there was a chance...

So she'd rushed in, feeling dreadful, to find Nick beside the bed with Bailey curled up beside him.

Nick was reading aloud, *Anne of Green Gables*, Gran's favourite book of all time. It wouldn't be hard to guess it, for the book had been lying on the bedside table, practically disintegrating with age.

She'd stopped short and Nick had smiled at her, but fleetingly, and he hadn't stopped reading until he reached the end of the chapter.

'I guess that's all we have time for tonight, Mrs Lawrence,' he'd said as he drew to a close. 'Misty'll take over now. Bailey and I will leave you while she says goodnight.'

Who knew what Gran had been able to understand, but Nick had read to her, and for now it felt right that he take her into the hospital to say goodbye.

'Thank you,' she told him as he drove.

'It is my very great honour,' he said. 'This is a privilege.'

* * *

The next few days passed in a blur. Too many people, too much organization, too great a bruise on her heart to take in that Gran finally wasn't here. If she'd had to do this by herself...

She didn't. Nick was with her every step of the way. That first night she clung and he held her. If Nick had carried her to his bed she would have gone. But...

'I don't want you to come to me in grief,' he said softly. 'I'll hold you until you sleep.'

'You're stronger than I am.' She tried for a chuckle. 'If you think I can lie beside you and sleep...'

'Okay, maybe it's not possible,' he said and tugged her tight and kissed her, strong, warm, solid. 'So separate bedrooms still.'

'Nick...'

'No,' he said, almost sternly. 'I want all of you, Misty. When you come to me it's not to be because you're raw and vulnerable. It's because you want me.'

'I do want you.'

'For the right reasons?' He set her back, tilted her chin and his smile was rueful. 'Loving you is taking all my strength but I won't go back on what I promised. I won't rush you.'

He was stronger than she was. There was nothing she wanted more than to lie with him, to find peace in his body, to find her home…

And she knew, as he turned away, that he sensed it. That she was torn.

There was still a part of her that wasn't his.

She and Gran had a contact point for her mother— a solicitor in London. A postcard had arrived about five years ago, adding an email address, 'In case anything ever happens'. She emailed her mother the morning Gran died. She left messages with the solicitor but she heard nothing.

So what was new? She went about the funeral arrangements and she could only feel thankful that Nick was with her. He didn't interfere. The decisions were hers to make, but he was just… there. His presence meant that at the end of a gruelling time with the funeral director she could stand in Nick's arms and let his strength and his warmth comfort her. She wasn't alone.

The funeral was huge—Gran had been truly loved. Misty sat in the front pew, and who cared what people thought, Nick sat beside her.

She spoke at the ceremony, for who else was to

speak for Gran? When she choked at the end, it was Nick who rose and held her.

This was the end of a life well lived. She couldn't be too sad that Gran was finally gone. But what did make her desperately sad...

Where was her mother?

She remembered her grandfather's death, terrifyingly sudden, her grandmother devastated.

'But your mother will come home now,' Gran had whispered, her voice cracked with anguish, and Misty knew she was searching for something that would lighten this awful grief.

'I expect she will,' she said, but of course she didn't.

So why should she come now?

If Nick hadn't been here...

All through that long day, as neighbours came, hugged her, comforted her, Nick was beside her, ready to step in, ready to say the right thing, ready to touch her hand, to make sure she knew he was there for her.

The locals responded to it. Nick had been here for little more than a month, yet already he was treated as one of them. He was Misty's partner. Misty's man.

If he wanted to marry her she'd say yes, she

thought, as the day faded to dusk. It might not be the right thing to think on this day but it steadied her. She had Nick and Bailey and two dogs and a house, and a job she loved and a town full of people who loved her.

Her house was full of food and drink, full of people who'd loved Gran. There was laughter and stories and tears, all about Gran.

'I keep thinking about Paris,' someone said—it was an old lady Misty scarcely recognised. And then she did. This was Marigold, her grandmother's bridesmaid. She remembered Marigold visiting them when she'd been a child. Marigold lived in Melbourne now, with her daughter. That she'd come so far to say goodbye to her friend made her want to cry.

'Paris?'

'Before we were married,' Marigold said. 'Your grandmother and I scraped enough to buy tickets on a ship and just went. Our parents were horrified. Oh, the fun… Not a bean between us. We got jobs waitressing. We taught each other French. We had such adventures. The night we both got bedbugs… There were two lovely English boys who let us use their room. They slept on the floor so we could have clean mattresses but the scandal when Madame found out where we'd slept; you'd have thought we were worse than bedbugs.'

Her old face wrinkled, torn between laughter and tears. 'Such a good friend. Such memories. Memories to last a lifetime.'

'Gran went to Paris?'

'She never let me tell you,' Marigold said. 'She told your mother and look what happened.' Then she glanced at Nick with the unqualified appreciation of a very old lady for a piece of eye candy. 'I can tell you now, though,' she said. 'You wouldn't leave this to racket around the world like your mother. This is lovely.'

For some reason, Misty was finding it hard not to cry. Why now, when she'd held it together all day? 'I...'

'Misty's had enough,' Nick, interceding gently. 'Today's been huge. If you'll excuse her...'

'That's right; you look after her,' Marigold said approvingly. 'She's a good girl, our Misty. She always does the right thing.'

The crowd left. Nick started clearing the mess but he shooed Misty to bed. The dogs were on her bed, warm and comforting, but she felt cold.

Gran had gone to Paris?

And then…the sounds of a car arriving. She glanced at her bedside table—eleven o'clock? What? Bailey had wanted to stay with Natalie tonight. Was something wrong? Had Natalie's parents brought him home?

She heard a car door banging. Nick's greeting was cautious—not the greeting he'd give Bailey. She heard a woman's voice, raised in sharp query.

'Who are you? What are you doing in my house?'

She knew that voice.

It was her mother.

It took her five minutes to get her face in order; to get her thoughts in order, to get dressed and calm enough to face her mother. By that time, Grace was already in the kitchen, drinking coffee, dragging on a cigarette.

She looked older, Misty thought, but then why wouldn't she? How long since she'd seen her? Ten years?

She was wearing tight jeans and black boots to above her knees. The boots were stilettos, their heels digging into the worn wooden floor. She was too thin. Her hair was black—definitely not what Misty remembered. It was pulled up into a too-tight knot and tied with a brilliant scarf that dragged the colour from her face.

This was a new look mother. Grace had a new look every time she saw her. Not so hard when she left years between visits.

She saw Misty in the doorway, stubbed her cigarette out and rose to embrace her. 'Misty. Sweetheart. You look awful.'

'Mum.' The word was hard to say.

Nick was standing beside the stove, silently watchful. He'd obviously made Grace coffee. He motioned to the kettle but Misty shook her head.

Her mother was here.

'Why have you come?' she asked, maybe not tactfully, but the emotions of the last few days had left her raw and unable to do anything but react instinctively.

'I was in Australia, darling, when the lawyer contacted me. In Perth.' Her mother sat down again and lit another cigarette. 'Wasn't that lucky?'

'How long have you been in Australia?'

'About a year.' A careless wave of the cigarette. Took had emerged from the bedroom to check out this new arrival. The cigarette came within inches of her nose and Took retreated.

Misty felt like doing the same.

A year…

'I let you know about Gran's strokes,' she said. 'I contacted the lawyer every month saying how ill she was.'

'Yes, but there was nothing I could do. Hospitals are not my scene. It was bad enough with Dad.'

'You only visited Grandpa for ten minutes. Once.'

'Don't you get preachy, miss,' her mother said tartly. 'I'm here now.'

'Not for the funeral. They're not your scene, either?'

Nick said nothing. He stood silent, wary.

'No,' her mother said. 'They're not. I can't pretend grief for someone I hardly knew. But I'm here now.' She glanced at Nick, considering. 'You two aren't in my bedroom, are you?'

'No.' Her mother's bedroom was on her side of the house. Beside hers.

'Excellent. No one told me you had a man.'

'I don't have a man. Nick's my tenant.'

'Some tenant.' She yawned. 'Such a long flight. I had to take a cheap seat. Did you know Fivkin and I have split? So boring. The money...you have no idea. But now...' She glanced around the kitchen thoughtfully and Misty suddenly knew exactly why she was here.

'I don't know any Fivkin,' she said, playing for time.

'Lovely man. Oh, we did such things. But now...' Her mother's face hardened. 'Some chit. He married her. Married! And the paltry amount he settled on me makes me feel ill. But that's okay. I'm fine. I've been checking out real estate prices here. We'll make a killing.'

'We?'

'Well, you and I,' Grace said, smiling tenderly at her daughter. 'The lawyer said I may need to give you a portion. You have been doing the caring, after all.'

It took only this. All of a sudden, Misty wanted to be ill. Badly.

'Leave it,' Nick said, and suddenly he was no longer on the sidelines. He was by Misty's side, holding her, his anger vibrating as a tangible thing. 'This is not the time.'

'To speak of money?' Her mother rose, too. 'I suppose you think I'm insensitive. It's just that I need to sort it and get away again. I've been stuck in Perth for too long. I hate keeping still. I talked to Mum years ago about selling this place but she wouldn't. Now…'

'Is there a will?' Nick asked. He was almost holding Misty up.

'I…yes,' Misty said.

'Whatever it says, it doesn't matter,' Grace told her. 'I'm the only daughter. Misty inherits after I go.'

'Misty's going to bed,' Nick said, cutting across her with brutal protectiveness. 'We'll talk this through in the morning.'

'We?'

'You fight Misty, you fight me,' he said.

'I'm sure Misty doesn't want to fight. She's a good girl.'

She *was* going to be ill. Seriously. If she stayed here…

'We're going,' Nick said, ushering her through the door. 'Look after yourself, Grace. Misty's had a terrible few days and she's exhausted. I need to look after your daughter, and I will.'

She'd thought she was shivering before. Now… She couldn't stop. Her whole body shook. Nick held her and swore. Or she thought he swore.

She didn't actually recognise the words but he kept right on until finally what he was saying cut through her shock and misery.

He was definitely cursing—but not in English.

She let it be for a while, letting the string of invective wash over her, finding it weirdly comforting. Being held by Nick and listening to…

'Russian?' she managed at last, and he said a few more carefully chosen terms of obvious invective.

Distracted, she pulled away. 'What are you saying?'

'What do you think I'm saying?'

'Swearing?'

'A nice boy like me?'

It was impossible to keep shaking when he was smiling. 'A nice boy like you,' she said, and she found herself smiling back. 'Definitely swearing.'

He tugged her back again, into his arms. Against his heart. 'Don't stop me,' he said. 'Otherwise I'm going to have to slug your mother and it's already been a black day. Ending up in jail might put the cap on it.' He waited until she was nestled against him again. He rested his chin on her hair and swore again.

'What is that?' she managed.

'Something a good girl shouldn't listen to.'

She choked. 'Language?'

'Tajikistan,' he said. 'It has the best cusses. Uzbekistan's good and so's Peru. Mozambique's not bad and Kazakhstan adds variety but, when I'm really against it, good old Tajikistan comes up trumps every time. Tonight's definitely a Tajikistan night.'

'That's my yurt territory.'

'Yurts and swear words. A truly excellent country.'

How could you not smile at yurts and Tajikistan swear words? She was almost forced to chuckle. Oh, but Grace…'She's appalling,' she whispered.

'She is appalling. Is there a will?'

'Yes, but…'

'Leaving her the house?'

'Leaving me the house.'

'You want me to evict her tonight? It'd be my pleasure.'

'No.'

'I could set the dogs on her,' he said thoughtfully,

and once again shock and sadness gave way to laughter.

'Right. And they'd evict her how?'

'Wind,' he said. 'If you're in a small enclosed place they can clear a room at twenty paces. All we do is ease them into her room and lock the door.'

She smiled again, but absently. 'She'll win,' she said. 'She has the right.'

'To this house? No, she doesn't. But it's okay, Misty. I'll manage this. This is our home.'

Our home.

The words had been swirling round for weeks. Our home.

He held her tight and let the silence soak in his words.

Our home.

Her home and his. And Bailey's and Ketchup's and Took's.

Home.

'It's okay,' he said again, and he stroked her hair and then he kissed her, first on the top of her head and then on her nose—and then more deeply on her mouth. He was tilting her face, holding her to him, but with no pressure. She could step away at any time.

The night was far too bleak to step away.

Nick. What would this day have been without him?

He loved her and she knew it. This man could make her smile when her world was shattered. How lucky was she that he was here?

She wanted him.

And, with that, everything else fell away. The sadness, the shock, the anger. There was only Nicholas, holding her, loving her.

There was only Nick.

'Can you take me to your bed?' she whispered and she felt his body still.

'Misty…'

'My mother will be sleeping next door. I don't want to sleep so close. Please…Nick, tonight I want to sleep with you.'

'I can't…' he said and she knew exactly what he was thinking. He couldn't hold her all night and take it no further.

'Neither can I,' she whispered and somewhere a chuckle came; somehow laughter was reasserting itself. 'Not any more. I want you, I need you and unless you don't have condoms…'

'I have condoms.' He sounded dazed. 'You

think I'd enter a house you were in without condoms?'

'I do like a man who's prepared.'

'Misty...'

'You've been wonderful,' she said, but suddenly he was holding her at arm's length.

'No,' he said, suddenly harsh. 'Not that. I'm not accepting an offering, Misty. Do you want me?'

'I...yes.' There was nothing else to say.

'Then this is mutual lovemaking, or not at all. I want you more than life itself, but I won't take you as thanks.'

'I do want you.'

'For love? This needs to be an act of love, Misty, or no matter that it'll tear me in two, it's separate beds. You've had an appalling day. Is this shock and grief talking? Or something else? Something deeper.'

Something deeper?

Her world was changing. It had changed when Gran died, she thought, and it had changed again when her mother walked in. But now... Something was emerging she wasn't aware she had. Herself. Misty. She had rights, she thought. This was her life.

And Nicholas was her man?

She took his hand, lifting it, resting it against her cheek. He let her be, not moving, letting her make her own declaration as to what she wanted. The back of his hand was against her cheek. She loved the feel of it. The strength.

Nicholas.

She did want. She ran her fingers across his face, a wondrous exploration, never letting her eyes move from his.

'Definitely deeper,' she whispered. 'I need to be kissed. More, I need to be loved, and I need to be loved by you.'

He gazed down at her for a long moment. He smiled, that magical heart-twisting smile—and then he kissed her.

Magically, his mouth was merging with hers. His hands were holding her face, brushing her cheeks with his lovely long fingers, loving her.

Loving her with his mouth.

The awfulness of the day disappeared as the kiss deepened, then deepened still more. She clung to him, aching to be held, aching to lose herself in love. Nicholas...

But he wasn't completely done with her. Not

yet. He moved back then, just a little, and his eyes were dark with love and desire.

'Misty, love, are you sure?'

She smiled at that, for she'd never been so sure of anything in her life. This moment. Nicholas.

'Yes.'

Definitely yes.

And the word was no sooner formed before she was being kissed again, lifted, held, claimed. Holding her in his arms as if she were a featherweight. A man triumphant with his woman.

'My bedroom,' he said, and she hardly recognised his voice. It was shaken with passion and desire. It was deep and husky and so sexy she wanted to melt.

But not here. Not yet. He walked to the door, still carrying her. Paused. Listened.

They heard a clatter in the kitchen—Grace was still there, then. They could make their way through the darkened passage, through the dividing door, then into Nick's side of the house.

Nick's bedroom was vast. The bed was a big four-poster with too much bedding and too many pillows. It was a bed made for more than one man.

It was a bed made for a man and a woman, and she wanted to be in that bed.

Nick was kissing her as he carried her. Then he was kissing her as he set her down on the bed. As he undid the buttons of her blouse. As he held her and held her and held her, closer and still closer.

She closed her eyes, aching with sensual pleasure. His fingers were tracing the contours of her body, her breasts. Each tiny movement sent shivers of wonder from top to toe.

She clung to him as he kissed her, holding him, glorying in the strength of him, the sheer masculinity, the wonder of his body. This day had seemed unreal. Now she wanted reassurance that this was happening in truth.

Her blouse was gone, and so was her bra. Nick was still clothed, but she could feel the strength of him underneath. In a moment she'd attack the buttons of his shirt, she thought. In a moment. When her body had space between trying to absorb the sensations she was feeling.

They had all the night. They had all the time in the world.

'I think I love you, Nicholas Holt,' she told him. 'Is that scary?'

He pulled away at that, holding her at arm's length. 'You think you love me?' he queried.

'I guess I know.'

'That's very good news.' His voice was grave, serious, husky with passion. 'For I know I love you. I'd marry you tomorrow. I will marry you tomorrow.'

Tomorrow.

The word gave her pause. Tomorrow. Grace. The worries that crowded in.

Nick sensed her withdrawal. He cursed in Tajik. 'Hey, Misty, don't look like that.'

'Tomorrow's tomorrow,' she murmured. 'Can we just take this night?'

A flicker of doubt crossed his face, and she smoothed it away with her fingers. 'No,' she said. 'This is not some one-night stand. I'm not saying that. I'm saying I do love you. I want you. Whether I want to marry you tomorrow...'

'It could be the day after.'

'It could,' she said and chuckled and tugged him close because she didn't want him to see doubt. She didn't want anything to interfere with tonight.

For tonight there was only Nick.

He still had clothes on.

'Not fair,' she said, and started slowly unbuttoning. He was hers, gift packaged, and she was going to take her own sweet time unwrapping.

Only maybe not. For, as she was concentrating—or trying to concentrate—on buttons, he was kissing her. Slowly, sensuously, achingly beautiful. Her neck, her lips, her eyelids.

She felt herself arch up to him and felt his fingers cup the smooth contours of her breasts, tracing the nipples, just touching, feather-soft, making her gasp with need and love and heat.

The night was magic. The moon was full outside, sending ribbons of silver over the ocean, the ribbons finding their way into the bedroom, across the bed, giving two lovers all the light they needed.

Only she had to get these buttons off!

She ripped.

'Uh oh,' he said.

'Was that a good shirt?'

'My best.'

'Sorry,' she said and her mouth found his nipples and suddenly any discussion of the ripped shirt was put aside.

He was hers, she thought. One loving gesture

and she had him, putty in her hands. Or in her mouth.

His breathing was ragged, harsh, as her fingers found his belt, unfastened, unzipped. She could hear his breathing deepening. She kissed his neck, tasting the salt of him.

He'd marry her. Her Nick.

Her fingers sought and found. Explored.

Loved.

Enough. One ragged gasp and he surrendered—or not. His hands caught hers, locked them behind her, and suddenly she was his again, and it was she who was surrendering. He kissed each breast in turn, tantalizing, teasing. Savouring. Their heated bodies moulded together.

Skin to skin.

Their mouths were joined again. Of course. It was as if this was their centre—where they needed to be.

Or maybe… Another centre beckoned. His hands were below her waist and she felt her jeans slipping.

As everything else slipped. Doubts. Sadness. Anger.

This night…this time… It was a watershed. Somehow, what was happening right now was firming who she was. A woman who knew what she wanted.

She wanted Nick, and wondrously he wanted her right back. How cool—how magical—how right!

But…

'Wait,' he said, in a voice she no longer recognised. 'Wait, my love.'

She must, but it nearly killed her to wait, until he'd done what he needed to do to keep them safe.

But then there was nothing keeping them apart. The night was theirs.

Outside, the world was waiting but for now, for this night, for this moment, there was only each other.

They were lying against each other, their bodies curved against each other, skin against skin. She'd never felt like this. She'd never dreamed she could feel like this.

A rain of kisses was being bestowed on her neck, her breasts, her belly, while his magical hands caressed and caressed and caressed. The heat…

The French windows were open. The warm night air did its own caressing, and the soft murmur of the surf was more romantic than any violin. She could vaguely hear the distant chatter of the ring-tailed possums who skittered along the eaves. She'd never felt so alive and so aware and so…beautiful?

But…hot? Oh, these kisses. The sounds of the night were receding, giving way to a murmur in her ears that was starting to grow.

He was kissing her low, loving her body, his tongue doing crazy, wondrous things… Amazing things.

'Nick!'

'Hey,' he growled and chuckled his pleasure and did it again. 'You like?'

Did she like? She arched upward, close to crying, aching with need. He was above her, sliding up again so his dark eyes gleamed down at her in the moonlight. He was loving her with his eyes.

'You want me?' he murmured and what was a girl to say to that?

'Like life itself,' she managed and she held him and tugged him down. Down…

But he wasn't sinking. His arms were sailor's arms, muscled, too strong for her to fight him. He was forcing her to wait. She arched and moaned and he kissed her, deeply, more deeply still. Holding the moment. Savouring what was to come.

'My Misty,' he whispered. 'My heart.'

'I need you. Nick, please...' Her thighs were burning; her body was on fire, but still he resisted. He lowered himself, a little but not enough, just so his chest brushed lightly against her breasts. He kissed her neck, behind her ears, her throat, her eyelids, and all the while his body brushed her breasts, over and back until she thought she'd melt with desire and love and need.

No more. What use would she be to this world if she melted into a puddle of aching need, right here on the bed? She took his shoulders and tugged, fierce with want, strong with need, and she rose to meet him.

And he was there.

Her love.

Her Nick.

Her body took rhythm from his. He was reaching so deep inside her, to the point where love and desire and need melted into one and she felt as if she were dissolving, dissolving, flying.

The night and the moonlight and the sounds of the sea, the grief of the day, the shock of the night, the luxury of this bed, the feel of this man's body... There was no separate sensation. No separate thought.

There was only her love.

And when finally they lay back, exhausted, as his arms cradled her and she moulded to his body and she felt his heartbeat, she knew her safe haven—her home—was much more than it had ever seemed.

Nick wanted to marry her. It was a tiny thought at the edge of all the consciousness she had left, but it felt lovely.

Their bodies could merge over and over. She could lie with this man for the rest of her life. She could help him raise his son, a little boy she loved already.

Wife and mother...

It felt... It felt...

'Like a miracle,' Nick said and he kissed her softly, languorously, lovingly. 'My Misty. At last I've come safe home.'

Safe home.

They were the last words she heard as she drifted into sleep.

Safe home.

CHAPTER TEN

MISTY stirred, stretched, opened her eyes. Sunbeams were streaming through the windows, falling across the rainbow quilt on the bed. Morning?

She'd slept spooned in the curve of Nick's body. Now she could no longer feel him. Oh, but she was so warm. Sated. She rolled over to find him. The grief she'd felt for Gran had eased, backed off, taken its rightful place. She was no longer bereft and grey. Nick…

Nick's side of the bed was empty.

The bedside clock said ten. What was she thinking? Her mother had to be faced. Life had to be faced.

Was Nick out there, facing it for her?

She showered fast, in Nick's bathroom because she didn't want to be caught by her mother, tousled by sleep, fresh from lovemaking. Besides, she liked the smell of Nick's soap. It smelled like Nick. Of course it did. So much for distinctive aroma, she thought wryly. Lemon grass? She'd thought it was testosterone.

She chuckled. Feeling absurdly happy even though Grace was out there—and that was a scary thought—she twisted a towel round her hair, donned Nick's dressing gown—a gorgeous crimson robe that looked as if it had come from somewhere exotic—of course it had come from somewhere exotic—and scuttled along the passage, through to the other side of the house to find fresh clothes.

And then she paused. There were voices coming from the kitchen. Her mother. Nick.

She should dress before she faced her mother, but...

She hesitated. The kitchen door was almost closed, but not quite. If she stood silent, she could hear every word.

Why would she want to?

She did.

'How much?' It was Nick's voice, but it was a tone she hadn't heard before. He sounded harsh and angry, trying, she thought, for control.

And her mother named a sum that made her gasp.

What the...? They were discussing...

She knew suddenly, definitely, what they were discussing. Selling her house.

'It's Misty's home,' Nick said. 'Her grandmother left it to her.'

'Misty's grandmother was my mother. This house is my right. I'll take her to court if I must but I won't need to. Misty will do the right thing. She always has.'

'You mean you expect her to walk away and leave you to do what you want?'

'I mean she'll do what's expected of her.' Her mother sounded scornful. 'You don't know her father. I did. He was a doormat. Misty's the same. Useful, though. She's kept this place looking great.' She could almost sense Grace assessing the place, looking around at the warm wood, at the lovely old furnishings. 'It'll get a good price. Much more than you're offering. So tell me again why I should accept?'

'Because Misty and I wish to live here. It's our home.'

'You're marrying her?'

'Yes.'

'Well, good for you. So buy it outright. Give me market value. Save your wife the nasty business of the courts. That'd upset her, fighting me in the courts.'

'It would or I wouldn't suggest it,' Nick snapped. 'You know she's a soft option. She's had no experience of the real world.'

'Then pay,' her mother said harshly. 'Of course you can't expose her to the courts. My mother always said she had to be protected. Don't tell her about what you're doing,' she said. 'It'll upset her. And here you are, ready to keep on keeping her safe. Excellent. Nasty thing, reality.'

'I'll get an independent valuation…'

'You'll take my price or I'll see Misty in court.'

She almost burst in on them then. Almost. Right at the last, she pulled back.

And here you are, ready to keep on keeping her safe.

Last night hadn't been about keeping her safe. Last night had been about loving her, pure and simple.

Did loving involve keeping her safe?

Last night she'd been so sure, but now…

She's a soft option. She's had no experience of the real world.

Standing in the passage, listening to her mother

produce valuations of like properties, listening to Nick become reasonable, as if what her mother was suggesting was reasonable, suddenly certainty gave way to doubt.

Nick was doing this to protect her. She knew it. So why did it seem so wrong?

Her mother's words…

You don't know her father. I did. He was a doormat. Misty's the same.

Anger came to her aid then. She was no doormat. How could Nick simply accept that as fact?

She's had no experience of the real world.

Nick wasn't going to pay for her house. Hard cold fact. She could go in there right now and tell him so. But something inside her was saying, *think. Get this right before you fly in with temper.*

She backed out of the passage, out of the back door to the veranda. Ketchup and Took were out there in the morning sun, supervising the sea. She sank down beside them and they nosed her hands and wagged their tails.

'Why aren't you in there biting my mother?' she whispered. 'Dogs are supposed to protect their masters.'

But the dogs weren't in the kitchen because

they'd found each other. Their security was each other.

As her security was Nick?

The dogs had had their adventures. They'd come home.

They weren't doormats.

Nick had had his adventures. Even Bailey...

She's had no experience of the real world.

Even her grandmother, never telling her she'd been to Paris because Misty had to be protected. Protected from herself?

There was a huge muddle of emotion in her mind but it was getting clearer. She stared out over the bay she'd loved all her life. The dogs nestled against her and the knot of confusion in her heart settled to certainty.

A doormat. Safe.

'You guys don't need me,' she whispered. 'When Gran was alive, when Ketchup needed me, and when I met Nick, my list seemed wrong. Stupid. But maybe it's not stupid. Maybe it's important if Nick and I are to build something. I won't have him spending his life thinking I need to be safe.'

Ketchup whimpered a little and put a paw on her knee. She managed to smile, but she didn't feel like smiling. What she was thinking…? It would hurt, and maybe it would hurt for ever.

'You don't really need me, do you?' she told Ketchup. 'You have Took. What's more, you have Nick and Bailey. You have guys who are in the business of keeping everyone safe. That's what they want to do, so they can stay here and do it.'

Okay. She took a deep breath. She girded her loins—as much as a girl could in such a bathrobe. She thought of what she had to do first.

'Nick's keeping this place safe. He can keep doing that, only there's no way he's paying my mother for the privilege,' she told the dogs.

She closed her eyes, searching for courage. What she was going to do seemed appalling. Loving Nick last night had made it so much harder.

She thought back to Frank, to her bitter colleague, regretting for all of his life that he'd never left this town.

'I can't do that to Nick,' she whispered. 'I'd try not to mind, and mostly I wouldn't, but every now and then…'

Every now and then she would mind, and it could hurt them all.

She's had no experience of the real world.

So do it now or do it never.

Deep breath. She stood and wrapped Nick's gown more tightly round her.

'Wish me luck, guys,' she whispered. 'Here goes everything.'

Nick had trouble with his own parents. Grace, though, was unbelievable.

She'd dumped her infant daughter on her parents and walked away. Half an hour with her this morning and he understood why. There was nothing she wouldn't do to get her own way.

If he hadn't been here…Misty would be trampled, he thought. Misty was no match for this… He couldn't find words to describe her. Not even Tajikistan had a good one.

'I have good lawyers,' Grace snarled and he faced her with disgust.

Maybe a fight through the courts would give the house to Misty, but the thought of it not succeeding, and the thought of what Misty would go through to claim it…

She might not even try. Misty was a giver, and he loved her for it.

'We need to get this in writing…' he started but

he didn't finish. The back door slammed open. Misty.

She was standing in the doorway, his crimson bathrobe all but enveloping her. The towel around her hair was striped orange and yellow. Her eyes matched her outfit. They were flashing fire.

'What do you think you're doing?' she demanded and she was talking to them both.

Grace stubbed her cigarette out in her saucer and smiled at her daughter, a cat-that-got-the-cream smile that made Nick feel ill.

'We're discussing business,' she said sweetly. 'Your man's being very reasonable. There's no need for you to get involved.'

'Nick's not *my man*.'

Uh oh. Nick sensed trouble. Where was the woman who'd melted into his arms last night, who'd surrendered completely, utterly, magically? The look she gave him now was one of disbelief. 'You're offering to buy *my* house. From my mother.'

'We want to live here.'

'So?'

'It's easier, Misty. I'll just pay her and she'll leave.'

'She's leaving anyway,' Misty snapped. 'Grace,

get out of my house. Now.' She picked up the ash-filled saucer and dumped it in the bin. 'You light up one more cigarette in this kitchen and I'll have you arrested for trespass.'

'This is my house.' Grace looked as stunned as Nick felt. This wasn't Misty. This was some flaming virago they'd never seen before.

'You left this house when you were eighteen,' Misty told her, cold as ice. 'You came back only when you needed money—or to dump a baby. What gives you the right to walk in now?'

'They're my parents,' Grace hissed. 'This house has always been waiting...'

'For you to sell it the moment they're dead? I don't think so. Gran left me this house, and its contents.'

'I'll contest...'

'Contest away,' Misty snapped and Nick could hear unutterable sadness behind the anger. 'Gran had macular degeneration for the last fifteen years. That's meant she's been almost blind. Since I was sixteen I've been signing cheques, taking care of all the business. Grandpa left Gran well off but almost all her income has been siphoned to you. You've been sending pleading letters. I've read them to her and every time she'd sigh and say,

"What shall we do, Misty?" To deny you would have killed her. So I've sent you cheques, over and over, and every single one was documented. You've had far more than the value of this house, yet you couldn't even find it in you to come to her funeral. I don't know what gene you were handed when you were born, but I thank God I didn't inherit it. Gran loved me. She wanted me to have this house and I will.'

'Misty…' Nick started and she turned on him then.

'And don't you even think of being reasonable. You're doing this to protect me? Thank you but I don't need protecting. I've had no experience of the real world? Maybe not, but I'm not going to get it with you protecting me. So I'm telling you both what's going to happen. First, Grace is going to get out. The cheques have stopped. You're on your own, like it or lump it. And Nick, you want a quiet life? That's what you can have because I'm leaving, too. Oh, not for ever, just for twelve months. I have a list to work through and for the first time in my life I'm free. I had Gran but she's dead. I thought I had Ketchup but he has Took and he has you. You and Bailey will love this house. It's safe…as houses.'

She took a deep breath, holding her arms across her breasts as if she needed warmth. He rose to go to her but she backed away. 'No. Please, Nick…' Her anger was fading a little but she seemed determined to hold onto it. 'This is hard but I have to do it. I know it sounds ungrateful, but…it's what I'm going to do. Now, I need to go and get dressed. Grace, when I get back here I don't want to see you. You'll be gone. Nick will be looking after my house—*my house*—but it's my house in absentia.'

They were left looking at each other. Grace looked…old, Nick thought and, despite the shock of Misty's words, he felt a twinge of pity.

Misty hadn't called her Mom or Mama or Mother. She'd called her Grace. If Bailey ever looked at him as Misty looked at Grace…

She deserved it. She'd been no mother to Misty, but still…

'You'd best go,' he said and Grace looked at him like a wounded dog.

'I don't…I can't. I don't have any money.' It was a defeated whine.

He hesitated. There'd been a resounding crash

from Misty's bedroom door. They were safe from her hearing.

Had Misty meant what she said?

Don't think about that now. Just get rid of Grace. Without Misty knowing?

Definitely without Misty knowing.

He tugged out his chequebook and wrote, and handed over a cheque. Grace stared down at it, stunned.

'I want the value of the house.'

'And instead I'm giving you your plane fare back to Perth and enough for approximately six months' rent. If Misty finds out I've done it I'll cancel the cheque. It's the last you'll get off us, Grace, so I suggest you take it and leave.'

'Us?' She dragged herself to her feet and regarded him with loathing. 'It didn't sound to me like there's any *us*. She sounds like she's leaving.'

'That's up to us,' he said evenly. 'But you're leaving first.'

Misty found him on the veranda, in his normal place, in his rocker, dogs at his feet. She was feeling ill.

She'd yelled at him. He didn't deserve to be yelled at.

'I'm sorry,' she said quickly before he could rise. 'That was dreadful. I sounded like I was a witch. You were only trying to help.'

'I'd like to help,' he said. 'You know I want to marry you.' He rose and came towards her. 'I'll protect you in any way I can.

'But I don't want to be protected. Nick, I'm sorry, but I don't want to marry you. Or…not yet.'

His face stilled. He'd taken her hands but she wouldn't let her fingers curl around his. She mustn't.

'I've never taken a risk in my life,' she said.

'That's why I love you.'

'You see, that's what I'm afraid of. I won't be loved because I'm safe.'

That he didn't understand was obvious. 'I don't love you just because you're safe,' he told her. 'I love you because you're beautiful and warm and big-hearted and fun and…'

'And safe. I'm someone to share a rocker with.'

'Misty…'

'It's okay,' she said, feeling unutterably weary.

She didn't want to say this. It would be so easy to sink into the rocker beside him, to wait until Bailey came home, to live happily ever after.

Was there something of Grace inside her? Some heartlessness?

No. She felt cold and fearful and sad, but she knew she was doing the right thing. If she didn't go now…She'd seen what bitterness could do.

'If you still want me in a year…' she said.

'A year?'

'I think I can do most of my list in a year.'

'What list?'

'It's a dream,' she said. 'I've had it since I was little. To fly away, to see something other than this town. Occasionally, when I was little, Grace used to send postcards, from one exotic place after another.'

'You were jealous of Grace?'

That was easy. 'I never was. Sometimes I even felt sorry for her. She'd fly in and make Gran cry and Gran would say the house was empty without her. But I kept thinking…why would you want to make Gran cry? That would have made me ill. I couldn't. Until now.'

His face was expressionless. 'So now you'll leave?'

'What's holding me here?'

'Us. Bailey and me.'

She closed her eyes. There was such a depth of meaning in the words—so much. He didn't understand. For her to walk away... To hurt him...

'See, that's the problem,' she said, as gently as she could. 'I'm falling so in love with you that I never want to hurt you. It's borderline now—that I never want to leave. As I could never leave Gran. For a while there I couldn't even leave Ketchup. But I must. Just for a year. Nick, can you try and understand?'

'Understand what? What do you want to do for a year?'

'Adventures,' she said promptly. 'I want to balloon over Paris at dawn. I want to roll down heather-covered hills in Scotland and get bitten by midges. I want to go white-water rafting in the Rockies...'

But she'd already lost him. 'You don't know what you're talking about,' he said coldly, flatly. 'You have everything you need here. It's...'

'Safe,' she threw at him. 'Tell me, if you didn't think I was safe, would you seriously consider marrying me?'

'No, but...'

'There you are, then.'

'But I have Bailey to consider.'

'You're not considering Bailey. You're choosing a wife for yourself. To choose me because top of your list of requirements is safe...Good old dependable Misty, cute as, we'll stay in her lovely house and if anything threatens her like a nasty, mean mother then we'll drive her away; we'll protect Misty because she's little and cute and can't protect herself.'

'This is overreacting.'

'Like paying for a house without even asking me?' she said incredulously. 'I guess I should be grateful, but I'm sorry, I'm not. You see, I want to be independent. Nick, I can't cling to you before I see if I can manage without anything to cling to. I need a year.'

'To go white-water rafting in the Rockies.'

'Yes.'

'You're just like Isabelle.' It was a harsh, cold accusation that left her winded.

She didn't answer. She couldn't. Was she just like Isabelle? Would she put a child's life at risk when she didn't need to?

If he thought that, then there was nothing to

defend. He wanted her to marry him and he didn't know the first thing about her.

She looked at him and her heart twisted. How easy would it be to fall into his arms, say sorry, it had all been a mistake and she wanted nothing more than to stay here with him, with Bailey, with Ketchup and Took, for ever and ever?

But he was looking at her with such anger.

Last night meant so much to her. It meant everything. But in a sense it was last night that had given her the courage to do this. For last night she'd accepted that she wanted to spend her life with this man, and she also knew that he deserved all she could give.

All or nothing. She would not marry him feeling like she did right now—knowing she'd dissolve into him and he'd make her safer, safer. She'd fought to get him onto a yacht. Every tiny risk would be a fight, but it'd be a fight to do what she already had now, and not what she dreamed of.

She couldn't let go of her dreams and marry him. She'd end up bitter and resentful.

She's had no experience of the real world.

It was a line to remember. It was a line to make her go.

'I will not end up in this rocker before I'm thirty,' she said, and suddenly she kicked the rocker with a ferocity that frightened them all. Took yelped and headed down the steps with her tail behind her legs. Ketchup yelped and cowered and cringed behind Nick's legs.

'Enough,' she said wearily. 'Sorry, guys. Sorry to you all. I know you're all very happy here. I hope you'll stay here and be safe and happy while I'm away. And if at the end of twelve months…'

'You expect us to wait for you?' Nick's voice was so cold she cringed. But she'd known this was the risk—the likely outcome. She had to face it.

'Can I ask whatever you do that you'll take care of Ketchup and Took?'

'Misty, after last night…' he said explosively and she nodded sadly.

'Yes. Last night was magic. It made me see how close I am to giving in.'

'Then give in.'

'I won't be married because I'm the opposite of Isabelle,' she said, and she knew it for the truth, the bottom line she couldn't back away from. 'You figure it out, Nick. I think I love you but I'm me. I'm me, lists and all.'

CHAPTER ELEVEN

'WHEN I suggested we get a relief teacher next term I thought you might use the time off for a honeymoon. Not to leave.' Louise was practically beside herself. 'What happened? We were all so sure. A honeymoon with Nick... Oh, Misty, why not?'

'Because our honeymoon would be at Madge Pilkington's Bed and Breakfast out on Banksia Ridge, with tea and scones, a nice dip in the pool every day and bed at nine. We might watch a bit of telly. Wildlife documentaries, maybe, but no lions hunting zebras for us. Nothing to put our blood pressure up.'

'You're nuts,' her friend said frankly. 'Nicholas Holt would put my blood pressure up all on his own.'

'Not if he can help it,' she said. 'Safe and sedate R Us, our Nick.'

'So you're definitely leaving?'

'I'm leaving.'

'Natalie's mother says he wants to marry you.'

'How would Natalie's mother know?'

'Does he?'

'He doesn't want to marry me,' she said. 'He wants to marry who he thinks I am. But, if I'm not careful, that's who I'll be and I suspect I'd hate her.'

'I don't understand.'

'You know something?' Misty muttered. 'Neither do I. But all I know is that I've fallen in love with him. He deserves everything I'm capable of giving and I don't know what that capability is. I have to leave to find out.'

'For ever?'

'For a year,' she said. 'I've taken a year's leave of absence. I'm not rich enough to walk away for ever. Nor do I want to.'

'He won't wait. You can't expect him to.'

'No,' she said bleakly. 'I can't expect him to.'

'Why is she going away?'

It was about the twentieth time Bailey had asked the question and it never got easier.

'Because her gran's died and she needs a holiday. Because we're here to look after the dogs.'

'We could all go on a holiday.'

'Misty wants to be by herself.'

But did she? He didn't know. He hadn't asked.

He wasn't going to ask. There was no way he was taking Bailey white-water rafting in the Rockies.

'We could go sailing,' Bailey said, verging on tears. 'All of us together.'

'You and I will go sailing. Next Saturday.'

'Misty's leaving on Friday.'

'Then we'll miss her very much,' Nick said as firmly as he could. 'But it's what she wants to do and we can't stop her.'

Friday. At eight Louise was collecting her to drive her to the airport. At dawn Nick went outside and found her crouched on the veranda, hugging two dogs.

'Hi,' he said and she turned to face him and he saw she'd been crying. 'Misty…'

'Hay fever,' she muttered, burying her face in Ketchup's coat. 'I'm allergic to dogs. How lucky I'm leaving.'

'Stay.'

'No.'

'Misty, we love you,' he said, feeling helpless. 'Both of us do. No, all of us,' he added, seeing the two dogs wuffle against her. 'This is craziness.'

'It's not craziness,' she said and swiped her cheeks with the back of her hand. 'It's what I need to do. I'm not Isabelle, Nick, no matter what you think, but I have my reasons. Instead of hating me for what I'm doing…I wish, oh, I wish you'd try to see who I really am.'

'I know who you are.'

'No, you don't,' she said and rose and brushed past him, heading for the door. 'You see what you want to see, and that's not me.'

'So who are you?'

'Heaven knows,' she said bluntly. 'I'm heading off into the unknown to find out.'

Nick watched her go.

He watched until Louise's car was out of sight.

Then he walked inside and slammed the door so hard it fell off its hinges.

Great. Something to do.

Something to do to stop him following her and dragging her back any way he knew how.

* * *

Misty was staring down at the receding vision of Sydney and all she could think of was what she'd left behind. What she'd given up.

'But I'm not giving it up,' she muttered. 'I'm leaving for a year. It'll be there waiting for me when I get back.'

'Nick won't be there,' she reminded herself. 'That's up to Nick.'

Oh, but what a risk. She sniffed before she could help herself and the man in the next seat handed over a wad of tissues.

'My wife does this every time we fly,' he said. 'So I come prepared. She's not with me this time but she sobbed at the airport. Leaving family then, are you, love?'

'Sort of.' It was all she could manage.

'He'll be there when you get back,' the man said comfortably. 'If he has any sense.'

'That's just the problem,' she told him. 'He has too much sense.'

'So what will we do without her?'

What, indeed? Move? The idea had appeal—to shift out of this house where he'd thought he had his life sorted. Only he had two dogs, and Bailey loved his new school, and to move out now…

They'd move before she came home, he decided. If she came home. She'd probably meet someone white-water rafting. Or kill herself in the process.

'Why do you keep looking angry?'

'I'm not angry.'

'So what will we do?'

It was Sunday afternoon. They'd had a whole forty-eight hours without her. It was raining.

Even the dogs were miserable.

Nick stared round the kitchen, looking for inspiration. 'Maybe we can cook,' he said. 'I've never tried a chocolate cake. You want to try?'

'It'd be better if Misty was here,' Bailey said, stubborn.

'Yes, but Misty's not here.' He headed for the recipe shelf and tugged out a few likely books. 'One of these…'

But then he was caught. There was a pile of scrapbooks wedged behind the recipes. One came out along with Mrs Beeton's *Family Cookery*.

It was a scrapbook, pasted with pictures. All sorts of pictures.

On the front in childish writing…

'Misty Lawrence. My Dreams, Book One.'

* * *

It didn't quite come up to expectations. Flying over Paris at dawn…

For a start, it was loud. It hadn't looked loud in the pictures. The brochures had made it look still and dreamlike, floating weightlessly above the Seine, maybe sipping a glass of champagne, eating the odd luscious strawberry.

She was cold. Champagne didn't cut it. If she wanted anything it was hot cocoa—where was Nick and his rocker now?—but she was too busy gripping the sides of the basket to even think about drinking or eating. The roar of the gas was making her ears ring. It was so windy… It had been a little windy before they'd started but had promised to settle, but a front had unexpectedly turned. So now they were being hit by gusts which, as well as making the ride bumpy and not calm at all, were also blowing them way off course.

Mind, she couldn't see their course. All she could see was a sea of cloud. The guy in charge was looking worried, barking instructions into his radio, most of which seemed to be about the impossibility of finding a bus to get his passengers back from who knew where they were going to land.

There were three couples in the basket and Misty. The couples were holding each other, giggling, keeping each other warm.

She was clinging to the basket, telling herself, 'Number One on my list, okay, not great, but now I'll get to wander down the Left Bank and take a barge down the Seine and buy Lily of the Valley on the first of May.'

Alone. She glanced across at the giggling couples who were holding each other rather than the basket.

Get a grip, she told herself. This was her list. She'd waited almost thirty years for it.

A month of Paris. Then the Dordogne. The great chateaux of Burgundy.

And then cruising the Greek Islands. It'd be fantastic—if she could just hold on for another hour and she didn't freeze to death or burst her eardrums. And maybe the clouds would part for a little so she could see Paris.

She must have started these lists when she was Bailey's age. They had all the scrapbooks out now, spread across Misty's kitchen table. Every night they seemed to be drifting back to Misty's side of the house to read her scrapbooks.

But, in truth, it wasn't just to read her scrapbooks. It felt better here—on Misty's side.

The dogs seemed more settled in Misty's kitchen. They slept by the stove, snuggled against each other, but every time there was a noise their heads came up and they looked towards the door with hope.

No Misty, and their heads sagged again.

How can they have fallen in love with her in so little time? Nick thought, but it was a stupid question. He knew the answer.

He had. And he was still falling...

They were reading the scrapbooks instead of bedtime stories. There was so much...

She'd been an ordered child, neat and methodical. The first couple of scrapbooks were exotic photographs cut from old women's magazines, and the occasional postcard. Some of the postcards had lost their glue and were loose. They were tattered at the edges as if they'd been read over and over. As he and Bailey flipped the pages it was impossible not to read their simple messages:

In Morocco. Oh, guys, you should be here. I feel so sorry for you, stuck in Banksia Bay. Grace.

He thought of an eight-year-old receiving this from her mother, and he thought of going out and cancelling Grace's cheque. He couldn't. It would have been long cashed. Grace was gone.

Misty was gone.

'I wish she was here,' Bailey said, over and over. He leafed through to the third scrapbook. 'This place is number one on her list.'

Her list...

They'd found it now, carefully typed, annotated, researched. What she'd done was take her piles of scrapbooks and divided them into twelve to make her list.

He went from scrapbooks to list, then back to scrapbooks. Pictures, pictures, pictures. And then, later, articles, research pieces, names of travel companies.

A child's hand turning into a woman's hand.

These were dreams, a lone child living with ailing grandparents, using her scrapbooks to escape to a world where her mother lived. Her mother didn't want her, but to know a little of her world... To dream of a world outside Banksia Bay...

I feel so sorry for you, stuck in Banksia Bay...

She'd been raised with that message ringing in her head.

Bailey found the scrapbooks entrancing but, as Nick worked his way slowly through them, he found them more than entrancing.

He began to see what he'd done.

He'd asked her to give up her dreams.

'Twelve months,' she'd said. 'I just want twelve months.' He hadn't given them to her. He'd reacted with anger.

'You're just like Isabelle.'

It had been said in an instinctive reaction when he hadn't got his way. Yes, it was born of his need to protect Bailey, but it had been unfair and untrue. He thought of Misty's face when he'd said it and he felt appalling.

'We miss her,' Bailey said, looking at pages linked to the item at the top of her list, at the advertisements for hot air ballooning over Paris, at the lists of castles on the Dordogne, at photographs of a tiny chateau hotel at Sarlat, at underground cellars, miles and miles of cellars where they kept the world's great Burgundies. Paris in springtime. France. 'She'll be there now,' he said. 'Is hot air ballooning dangerous?'

Yes, was his instinctive response. After the terrors Bailey had been exposed to…

But he knew it wasn't.

'No,' he told his son. 'It can be uncomfortable. Often noisy.'

'It doesn't look noisy,' Bailey said doubtfully.

'The gas burners are really loud.'

'I don't think Misty likes noise. Do you think we should ring her and tell her not to do it?'

He picked up the list and read it. Drinking Kir at sunset on the Left Bank. Wandering through the Louvre. Standing on top of the Arc de Triomphe and watching the crazy traffic underneath.

What was this? Hiring a motor scooter and riding round the Arc de Triomphe? Should he ring and tell her how crazy that was?

No.

He thought of her sailing, wearing a life vest. He and Bailey had watched her from the clubhouse before the race, practising and practising. Pushing herself to the limit, but her little boat was fine.

He'd accused her of being just like Isabelle. Was he mad?

'I think Misty wants to find out all by herself,'

he said, and he knew part of it was true—she did want to find out—but the rest…

Bailey went to bed and he returned to Misty's side of the house—with scrapbooks. Misty was here on these pages, a girl's dreams followed by a woman's serious commitment.

He'd given her a choice. Himself and his son—or her dreams. Would he want her to give this up?

He'd asked her to.

What to do?

He had clients arriving in Banksia Bay now. His international clients were talking to him about their boats, about their dreams. They were finding out where he was based and saying, 'You know what? We'll come talk to you in person.'

They loved it. Banksia Bay was beautiful. He never had to leave.

Bailey was safe.

But these scrapbooks…

Her list…

Twelve months.

The dogs sighed. They lay at his feet but they looked at the door.

'She'll be back in a year,' he told them.

But if there's someone else in her balloon…

some guy who sees what Misty really is...how beautiful...

How could they not? He flicked through the list, thinking if she found someone to do these with her...

It was an amazing list.

He hadn't done some of the stuff on this list.

Bailey was asleep. Here. Safe. But maybe... maybe...

He read the list again. Slowly. Thoughtfully.

This was not Isabelle.

Maybe dreams were made to be shared?

He turned to the dogs, considering. It was his responsibility to care for these two.

Kennels?

No. He knew where they'd come from. If he and Bailey were to be free...

'Sorry, guys, but I think tomorrow morning we need to go see Fred.'

Fred the vet.

She'd been away for six weeks. She was loving every minute of it. Sort of.

Number three on her list was cruising the Greek islands. It'd be magic. She'd pinned pictures up on her study wall at home. Whitewashed villas with blue-painted windows. Caiques bobbing at anchor. Greek fishermen stripped to the waist, hauling in their nets. Santorini, Mykonos, the Cyclades islands. It was all before her.

She climbed off the bus at the harbour in Athens. Her boat was due to leave in two hours.

Two emotions…

After so much planning, it was impossible not to feel exhilarated as dreams became real.

It was also impossible to block the thought that back home was Nick. Nick and Bailey and Ketchup and Took, learning to live in Banksia Bay without her.

She couldn't think about them now. She mustn't. To follow her dreams with regret—what sort of compromise was that? She lifted her back pack and trudged down to the departure point, telling herself firmly to think ahead.

But the boat at anchor wasn't what she'd expected. In the pamphlets it had been shown as a graceful old schooner, wooden planking, sails, lovely.

The boat before her was huge, white, fibreglass. There were tourists filing up the gangplank already. Many tourists. This was far bigger than she'd imagined.

Her heart sank—but she was getting used to this. Adjusting dreams to fit reality. She would *not* be disappointed. She'd looked forward to this for so long. Sailing on the Aegean…

But still… No sails. So many tourists.

A hand on her shoulder.

'It's not the same as your pictures. Maybe we can offer you an alternative?

She almost jumped out of her skin.

She whirled—and he was there.

'We came to find you,' Nick said before she could even kick-start her heart. 'Me and Bailey.' He smiled down at her, a smile that made her heart stop even trying to kick-start—and he put on the voice of a spruiker, the guys who pushed tourists to change their minds.

'Madam wishes to sail the Greek islands? On this?' He gestured contemptuously to the fibre-glass cruiser. 'My *Mahelkee* is a much smaller boat, but she's infinitely more beautiful. There's four aboard now. A crew of four, whose only wish is to keep madam happy. You come with us, madam, and we will make you happy. You come with us, madam, and we intend to make you happy for the rest of your life.'

CHAPTER TWELVE

You didn't travel alone for long without learning to avoid spruikers. Misty was very good at saying, 'No, thank you,' and walking away without looking back.

But this was some spruiker.

For a start, he wasn't alone. He was working as one of a pair. For as well as Nick with his heart-stopping smile, there was also Bailey. Bailey wasn't smiling. He was a little behind his father, gazing up at her as if he wasn't quite sure he still knew her. Anxious. Pleading?

Nick. Bailey.

How to get her heart beating like it should again? She wasn't sure she could.

'H…How…?' she managed. 'How did…?'

'Lots of work,' Nick said. He'd removed his hand from her shoulder. He was no longer touching her. He was just…smiling. If she wanted to back away and head up the gangplank to her cruiser, she still could.

Turn away? A girl would be mad.

'W…work?' she managed. 'You've worked to get here?'

'We just got on an aeroplane,' Bailey said from behind his father. 'It was easy.'

'So no work.'

'We would have worked if we had to,' Nick said. Virtuous. 'To reach you. And I had to make a whole lot of phone calls.'

'Dad slept on the aeroplane,' Bailey said.

'First class, huh,' she said and somehow she managed a smile.

'Of course,' Nick said, and his smile deepened and strengthened, a caress all by itself. 'If it's to reach you, then only the best will do.'

'Nick…'

'We have your list.' Bailey was clutching his father's hand but his eyes were on Misty. Desperately anxious. 'Dad and I have your list. We want to do it, too. If you let us.'

There was a statement to take a girl's breath away. *We want to do it, too…*

'I believe I've made a mistake,' Nick said gravely. Around them, passengers were streaming up onto the gangplank. They were having to divert around this couple and child, plus one very large backpack. Misty didn't notice. 'I believe I made the biggest mistake of my life. I'm hoping… Bailey and I are hoping…that it's not too late to fix it.'

She was having trouble breathing. 'I don't know what you mean,' she whispered.

'We mean your list is part of you,' Nick said, and still he didn't touch her. He was holding back, leaving her be, outlining the facts and allowing her space to absorb. 'After you left, Bailey and I read your scrapbooks.'

'You read…'

'We hope you don't mind.'

'No, but…'

'But they're part of who you are,' he said. 'Part of the whole. Misty, we tried to love only the part of you that I wanted. That was so dumb it doesn't bear thinking of. I'm hoping against hope that it's not too late to let me repair the damage. I'm hoping it's not too late to tell you that I love all of you, without reservations. That Bailey and I fell in love with Misty the schoolteacher, Misty the dog-lover, Misty the sailor. But we want more. We want Misty the traveller. Misty the adventurer.' He hesitated. 'And… And Misty, my wife?'

'Oh, Nick…'

'And Misty the mother,' Bailey piped up from behind. 'When we talked about this at home… Dad, you said Misty the mother. You said let's come over here and see if we can make Misty love us. Let's come over here and see if we can get Misty to teach me how to make scrapbooks. But I've already started,' he said proudly. 'I have a picture of a motorbike on the first page.'

'A motorbike,' Misty said faintly. 'Aren't they dangerous?'

'Yes,' Bailey said, peeping a smile. 'And they're noisy. Like balloons.'

She smiled back. She wasn't sure how she managed to smile. She believed there were tears slipping down her cheeks.

Tears? Who felt like crying now?

'We have a tour mapped out,' Nick said. He reached a hand towards her and then pulled it back again. As if he was afraid to touch—as if she might turn and flee if he did. 'Santorini, Mykonos, the Cyclades Islands.'

'They're the ones on your list but Dad says we can do more,' Bailey said. ''Cos *Mahelkee* is a smaller boat. She can go into lots of places big boats can't go. Dad showed me on the Internet— there's beaches and beaches and beaches. There's even places where Ketchup and Took can get off. They can't get off here because of…qu… Dad, what is it?'

'Quarantine,' Nick said, his eyes not leaving Misty's face. 'We had a friend sail *Mahelkee* here, and Ketchup and Took flew with us. Fred's given them every inoculation they need. If they stay on the boat when there's any restrictions then they can go with us wherever we want.'

'You've brought the dogs?'

'Family,' he said diffidently. 'They didn't want to stay at home.'

'You've brought two stray dogs to Greece?'

'Their inoculations will cover them for almost every place on your list. There's a couple of places they can't go, but Rose and Bill will look after them then.'

'Rose and Bill?'

'Isabelle's parents,' he said, and there was a tension in his voice that said he wasn't sure if he was stepping over some invisible line with this. 'They've been desperate to help since Isabelle died. They love Bailey. We've sort of…I've sort of backed off from them, but they're lovely people. They're Bailey's grandparents. I know they'll like you.'

'And they have a really big boat,' Bailey said. 'So they can look after Took and Ketchup every time we go and have adventures and then we can come back and get them. And Took's even learned to swim. Dad went swimming yesterday and Took jumped right in and swam as well—and they already know how to use their sand tray.'

'How long have you been here?' she asked faintly.

'Four days,' Nick said. 'Waiting for you.'

'Four days…'

'We'll wait for a year if we must. If you really want to do your list alone. Only we'd very much like to do it with you.'

'I want to see snow buntings,' Bailey said.

Oh, help. She was really crying now. She was crying and crying, and an elderly woman cast her a sideways look and stopped.

'Are you okay, dear?' she said. 'Is this man annoying you? Can I get my husband to carry your bags aboard?'

'I…' She had to pull herself together. Somehow. She sniffed and sniffed again. 'I'm fine,' she managed. 'I'm really fine. This gentleman's not annoying me at all. In fact…' She took a deep breath. Regrouped. Cast a last look at a big white fibreglass boat that was no longer about to carry her to her dreams.

'In fact, I might have found someone to carry my bags for me,' she managed, and she smiled. And then she smiled and smiled, and before the elderly lady knew what hit her she reached out and hugged her. 'But thank you for offering. I love it that you offered your husband, but I believe I might just have found my own.'

'You mean you'll let us join you?' Nick asked and the whole world held its breath.

Her world settled. Her heart started beating again. She was standing before the man she loved with all her heart, and her list was waiting.

'Why, yes,' she said as he reached for her and beside her an extremely astonished elderly lady started to smile as well. 'Why, yes, I believe I will.'

Sunrise.

Bailey was still in bed, deeply asleep. He'd had a really big day yesterday, trudging gamely up the sides of the hills of Tulloch. He'd seen snow buntings. He'd giggled and run and been every inch the child he should be.

He seemed younger now than he'd been twelve

months ago. That was great. It was how it should be. He was confident and happy. If he woke now, he had his dogs on his bed and the lovely lady who ran their bed and breakfast overlooking the loch would reassure him that Dad and Misty would soon be home.

But not yet. Bailey might have seen a snow bunting but Misty wanted to hear them, and there wasn't a lot of listening to be had with a chattering seven-year-old. So they'd crept away at dawn, rugged up, because even in summer the Highlands could be cool and misty.

They walked side by side up the scree, sometimes hand in hand, steadying each other, sometimes coming close, hugging, then clambering the tricky bits apart…and then coming together again as they intended coming together for the rest of their lives.

They reached the point the landlady had suggested. They sank into a bed of heather—not so soft as Misty had imagined—she did need to keep adjusting these dreams—and they watched the sun rise over the distant peaks.

In silence. Apart from the snow buntings.

It was the best…

Where had she read the words… *'It's not how*

many breaths you take; it's how often your breath is taken away'?

Her breath was taken away now. She was lying in heather on a Scottish hillside, listening to the birds she'd read about for so long, beside the man she loved.

Her husband.

They'd married in Greece, on the Isle of Lindos. In an ancient temple overlooking the Aegean Sea. Lindos hadn't been on her list but there'd been a few wonderful additions to her list and there were more to come.

'Does this place come up to scratch?' Nick asked her as the sun rose higher and the tangerine blush faded to the cool, clear grey of the day. 'Can we put a tick beside this one?'

'Yep,' she said and rolled happily into his arms. 'Yes, we can. Definitely a tick. Or maybe a scratch is a better description. Oh, Nick, I love you.'

'I love you, too,' he said and he kissed her long and wondrously and they clung and held—two lovers finding their dreams together. 'You want to go back to bed?' he asked as the kiss finally ended and she knew by the passion in his voice what he wanted—what they both wanted right now.

'Wuss,' she said. 'Just because heather's a bit scratchy.'

'A lot scratchy. Double bed back at the house. Pillows. More pillows. Lovely, soft quilt.'

'Take your coat off,' she ordered. 'Heather. More heather. Lovely soft coat.'

'Wicked woman. Someone might see.'

'We're the only people in the world,' she said and kissed him again. 'Don't you know?'

'We're not, you know,' he said and held her close. 'Misty, it's almost time we went home.'

Home. Banksia Bay. It was waiting for them, a lovely place to come home to.

But maybe not for ever. They'd leave and leave again, she thought. But for now…maybe they did need a bit of stability.

Banksia Bay was a good place to have a baby. Twelve weeks to go… She put her hand on her tummy and she felt her baby move, and she thought life couldn't get any better than it was right now.

'I'm thinking we should get another dog,' Nick said and she pushed herself up on her elbows and looked down at him. Dark and lean and dangerous. Wickedly laughing.

Her Nick.

'Why would we get another dog?'

'I've been thinking…'

'Thinking's risky.'

'Yes, but…' He tugged her down and kissed her nose. 'Ketchup and Took…in a way they brought us together.'

'I guess they did.'

'So to bring this new little person into the family…'

'We need another dog?'

'A pound dog,' he said in satisfaction. 'One who needs a home.'

'We'd have to extend the sand tray on *Mahelkee.*'

'I'm a marine architect,' he said smugly. 'Bigger sand tray? I can handle that.'

'Baby first,' she said. 'Dogs need attention.'

'Home first,' he said, unbuttoning her coat with delicious, languorous ease. 'Banksia Bay.'

'For now,' she said and kissed him and kissed him again, as she intended to kiss him for the rest of her life. 'Banksia Bay's our base. Somewhere Bailey can go to school, where we can work, where we can recoup for the next adventure. But home? Home's where the heart is. Home's number thirteen or number fourteen on our list. Home's wherever we are, my love. Home is where I am, right now.'

* * * * *

MILLS & BOON PUBLISH EIGHT LARGE PRINT TITLES A MONTH. THESE ARE THE TITLES FOR AUGUST 2011.

JESS'S PROMISE
Lynne Graham

NOT FOR SALE
Sandra Marton

AFTER THEIR VOWS
Michelle Reid

A SPANISH AWAKENING
Kim Lawrence

IN THE AUSTRALIAN BILLIONAIRE'S ARMS
Margaret Way

ABBY AND THE BACHELOR COP
Marion Lennox

MISTY AND THE SINGLE DAD
Marion Lennox

DAYCARE MUM TO WIFE
Jennie Adams